I ONCE HAD A MASTER
AND OTHER TALES OF EROTIC LOVE

I ONCE HAD A MASTER

AND OTHER TALES OF EROTIC LOVE

by John Preston

CLEIS PRESS

Copyright © 1984 by John Preston.

All rights reserved. Except for brief passages quoted in newspaper, magazine, radio, or television reviews, no part of this book may be reproduced in any form or by any means, electronic or mechanical, including photocopying or recording, or by any information storage or retrieval system, without permission in writing from the publisher.

Published in the United States by Cleis Press Inc., P.O. Box 14697, San Francisco, California 94114.
Printed in the United States.
Cover design: Scott Idleman
Cover photograph: Copyright © 2004 by Rick Castro, www.rickcastro.com
Text design: Frank Wiedemann
Logo art: Juana Alicia
10 9 8 7 6 5 4 3 2 1

*To
Samuel Steward
and
Frederick Brandt*

I Once Had a Master
1

Pedro
5

An Education
17

Transitions
31

An Hour's Stopover
43

Authenticity
63

Metamorphosis
79

Interludes
93

Escalation
105

Epilogue
On Writing Pornography
127

About the Author
143

I ONCE HAD A MASTER

I once had a master who lived far from the city.

Every Friday I would leave my job in an office building. I would take an express train to the next large metropolis and change there for a local. I would sit watching a progression of towns, each smaller than the last, speed by my window. At the terminus I would climb out and find him waiting. Every Friday he would be standing next to his truck. There would be no greeting from either of us; the ritual was so secure that it did not need the support of words.

As he drove away from the station I would begin the disrobing he would expect. There were times on hot summer nights that the wind caressed my bare chest with welcome cooling relief. But my comfort did not concern him, and there were other times in the winter when the draft would send chills through my body when my shirt removed the little protection it had provided. He did not care for my discomfort.

The removal of each piece of clothing marked the advance

of our journey. By the time he pulled into his own driveway I would be naked, sitting beside him in the truck, waiting to begin the weekend.

When he finally pulled into the space beside his house—actually no more than a cabin in the woods—I would have to make my way inside. He appeared ignorant of the freedom that my nudity represented on a summer night, and equally as ignorant of the danger it held on frozen winter evenings. His only concern was that I be without clothes in his house.

There was a ceremony every Friday evening. I would shower, but not to cleanse myself; that was unimportant. I would stand beneath a hot spray of water to let its moisture soften my body hair. Every Friday he shaved every inch of my skin below my neck. He could not tolerate even a few strands separating my skin from his touch.

For the weekend I became his servant. I would cook his meals, clean his house, wash his clothes, tend his garden, chop his firewood. I would do so always naked, always vulnerable.

He would tolerate no limitation to my service. The orifices of my body were open for him to take on a whim—my mouth, my ears, my ass, my hands were there whenever he had the desire to use them. He never let his physical wants fall into a pattern; he would take me while standing up cooking in front of the stove, or while working in the fields or even in the soundest of sleep.

We talked almost not at all. My ministrations were to his body. Not his fantasies nor his mind. I washed his torso while it sat in the bathtub. I massaged it in front of the fireplace. I took its relief in the fields.

He was never mindlessly cruel. But he would beat me greatly if my service ever faltered or if my mind wandered noticeably into a private world of daydreams. There was no time on these weekends for my self-indulgences. I was never allowed to resist punishment. To do so would be to threaten my right of attendance.

No other person ever came to his house while I was there, though I could not have stopped anyone. He did not want there to be another person to interfere with my growing vulnerability or his own growing control.

The weekends took on more meaning each time they were repeated. The few words that passed in the beginning began to disappear as time made them superfluous. The days between my journeys became less and less important.

It had not taken long for the trip back to the city to be dreaded. I would have to reverse the ritual of dressing as he drove me to the station. I had to be fully clothed by the time he parked in front of the iron rails.

The first summer I learned more about my body than in all the summers that had preceded it. I ran naked across flowered fields and sprawled my shaven skin in oceans of clover. I became fearless of my physical self. I took on color and my muscles toned as they worked hard on his farm. I welcomed every time he took me. I responded passionately to his assaults. I spread my jaws and my sphincter for him as he invaded my very being.

The first winter I learned more about my fear than I had ever known. I often sat down next to the stove to try to ease my naked coldness. My body and my self were captives of the house. I was desperately frightened of those times when he would force me to run without shoes through the snow to gather wood for the fire. He, himself, had no other outlet for his own physical being than to use my body. I received the onslaught of his frustration every weekend. I took the results of a winter's week's isolation every time I came to him.

But, always, the spring would begin and we were able to venture further out into the more welcoming sun until once again it would be summer and our selves and our bodies could rush through forests to find swimming holes to dive into and we could feel attached to nature.

I would love him in the summertime.

I would hate him in the winter.

I would always return as a pilgrim every weekend.

He never talked to me. He would listen when I professed my love. He would sit serenely while I begged for his response. He would let my anger glance off his brow if ever I dared to speak it. But he would never respond.

Finally I went to his farm no more. I was frightened that I would forget that he was not God.

PEDRO

When I was an adolescent, sex existed in a strangely isolated manner. It never happened with anyone I knew. Not only did I never have sex with my peers in high school, I hardly even contemplated them as possible partners. Sex happened when a stranger offered it. My only part in the foreplay was to learn to make myself available.

I grew up in rural New England. The easiest way to present myself for a potential seduction was to hitchhike. Like many other New England boys I spent untold hours thumbing aimlessly through Massachusetts waiting for the telltale hand that would finally dare to rest on my thigh.

Eventually I discovered Park Square in Boston and learned that I could encourage the older men to approach me by standing listlessly at certain corners. Eventually one of an army of traveling salesmen from Hartford or Albany or some other city would gather the courage to proposition me. I always went with him.

The encounters were never romantic. The men were most often nameless. Cocks were the only focus except for the occasional man who paid attention to one of our assholes and wanted to fuck or get fucked. I received a great deal of physical release from these genital adventures and I suppose got some validation for my homosexuality. Certainly the intense orgasms helped prove it was going to be a physically pleasurable part of my life. But little was done to lessen the grinding isolation of my shy teenage years. By the time I met Pedro I was eighteen or nineteen. I had the slightest veneer of sophistication earned from a year in college. I was home for summer and waiting for something to happen.

One of the most valuable things I had gotten from school was a fake ID. It opened up the world of gay bars. On my first weekend home I crossed over to Rhode Island and walked the streets of Providence until I found one. It was going to be many years before loud and glittering discos flaunted themselves. Gay bars then were on back alleys with plain unmarked doors or camouflaged in some other manner. The only way to locate one was to wander the downtown of a city and try to find some "obvious homosexuals," then shadow them until they piloted you to one of the secret places. That was what I did that night: a chattering pair of queens forged the path for me.

I had barely begun my first beer when Pedro introduced himself. He was quickly friendly. He had an arm around my shoulders within five minutes and had kissed my lips inside ten.

His aggressiveness would have excited me in any event, and it was further enhanced by his appearance. He was not handsome in any of the usual ways, but he was roughly masculine. He was a big man, easily over six foot. He was Portuguese and had the thick black kinky hair and heavy beard that are so lavish on those particular Latin men.

The arm that hung on my shoulder was bulky with both muscled and unmuscled flesh. There was a beginning of a paunch in the belly that pressed against me, but it was firm, not flabby. He was a truck driver.

I don't remember any conversation where it was actually decided that we would have sex. I would like to think it had been mutually assumed, but more likely Pedro simply told me it was going to happen and I acquiesced.

That was the first night I ever slept in another man's own bed—the only other times I had even had sex between real sheets had been in hotel rooms. It was also the first time someone kissed me while he fucked me.

These things would have been important by themselves. Something else struck me as even more noteworthy: Pedro's cock was big. But it oozed so much pre-cum that he could fuck me without any grease, and after the initial entry it was still painless. When he was buried inside me and my body was reacting with its spontaneous intensity I was able to come without even touching myself.

I could later realize that one fuck erased any lingering intellectual doubts about my sexuality. For whatever reason, I had clung to the need for an artificial aid for sex as the proof that it was somehow wrong. Pedro took that away from me and I never got it back.

Pedro assumed many things after that. I never questioned him. We became a couple. Our shared life was never clouded by hiding. Pedro was in his thirties and though I never asked much about his history he must have made a lot of decisions that I, never having an opportunity to challenge his actions, never had to make alone.

I was gay. I had a man who loved me. We were in love. Love was natural. We spent time together. We had sex. We never denied it—though we were never actually asked.

We were a couple always. Even my family had to know about it. They must have been aware of my sexuality before, but it had never been discussed. Now, because of Pedro they would never have the luxury of worrying about it. It was simply there.

Pedro would come by whenever he felt like it. There was never a warning phone call. It was only a forty-mile drive to my house from Providence and he'd often show up after work and announce he was taking me to dinner. My parents couldn't match him when he was smilingly arguing away their objections. He'd sometimes come later in the evening with a bottle of whiskey that he and my father would drink at the dining room table. If he thought my mother was becoming worried he'd bring her flowers.

Everyone knew that whenever Pedro knocked on the door he would eventually take me with him and not return me till the next morning. We never talked about that. It was simply one of Pedro's assumptions, and my parents' passivity in the face of the robust Portuguese's insistence matched mine.

They also loved him. He forced them to make a leap they never even contemplated. They had never thought of me in the context of having a male/male relationship, I'm sure. Now they were talking about Pedro to their friends. While they could never articulate the nature of who he was to me, they could somehow express real pleasure in Pedro and tell people how lucky I was to "have" him.

I could sense these things in my parents. I still wonder what the neighbors and relatives thought about the appearance of this man in my life. He certainly couldn't have made any sense to them. I was a tall skinny Yankee boy, a loner who shunned being one of the regular guys. I had spent all my years hiding behind books and ideas.

Now, standing awfully close beside me was a truck driver from Providence who not only was at least ten years older than I, but obviously had never gotten beyond high school. Pedro would drink with them. He spoke the same working-class dialect, even perhaps one a little rougher and a little more often punctuated with "fuck." He knew the names of every player on the Red Sox, the Bruins and the Celtics. No one could match his mechanical ability when it came to cars.

He broke their image of a regular guy in only one way: he would never talk about women. Beyond that he presented only one mystery: at the end of the day he left with a teenage boy in tow.

Little changed when we were alone, except for the addition of sex. He took it whenever he chose. I never denied him; I wouldn't have known how.

After he had a few drinks with my father, and as we were driving back to Rhode Island, his lust would sometimes overtake him. He'd pull over on the side of the road and unzip his fly and bring out his already erect cock. "Suck it."

He'd talk about his cock while I had it in my mouth. He'd tell me how it felt, and he'd instruct me to increase or decrease the speed of my motions or else to move my tongue against the head in some certain way.

Every once in a while he'd grab my hair and with a painful

jerk he'd drag me up away from his erection. "You really like it, don't you?" He'd not let go until I said yes. Then he'd guide my willing mouth back down over the shining shaft.

I don't think I ever slept in Pedro's bed without getting fucked at least once. Often it happened two, three, even four times in a night. I was never asked. He would simply manipulate my body into whatever position he wanted and his cock would enter me.

Wherever we went Pedro took care of me. He bought the drinks, carried the conversation, focused people's attention on me. He constantly worried if I was comfortable; he always searched for new ways to make himself the source of my pleasure.

It wasn't until we had been seeing one another for many weeks that I found out the extent of Pedro's passion. We were at a party in Pawtucket. It was early evening. About twenty-five men were on the patio of someone's house drinking and talking. One man was particularly interested in me. He found occasions to pat my ass and to touch me in other places. I was unused to the attention of this kind of stranger and enjoyed it; I didn't stop to think about Pedro. Then the man kissed me.

What followed happened quickly. People were yelling before I had understood it all. Pedro was standing beside me. His arm lashed out and the stranger collapsed on the floor. His nose was grotesquely broken. Blood gushed out from his face.

Pedro stood with his fists and jaw clenched with anger. His chest was quivering with his need to control himself. The only sound in the group, once the screams had stopped, were the coughing sobs of the man sprawled on the flagstones in front of us.

Pedro finally grabbed my arm and led me from the party. We didn't speak a word as he drove through the run-down Rhode Island tenement cities. When we got back to Providence he drove to his house; when he had parked we locked the car and walked inside.

Pedro had a favorite chair in a corner of his small living room. He went to it and sat down. He lit a cigarette. Only after he took the first drag did he talk to me. "Take off your clothes."

I stood in the middle of the room and stripped. I was surprised that I wasn't frightened of him. I concentrated instead on the sensation of disrobing in front of him and the excitement of having his eyes study my body as each piece of clothing was removed. By the time I was nude my cock was stiffly erect.

"Get on your hands and knees."

I did. I felt my scrotum being squeezed between my thighs. My cock's tip bounced against my belly. My eyes continued to study Pedro.

"Crawl over here."

I moved across the floor. The rug was harsh and the shuffling motions burnt my kneecaps. I kept on going until my head moved into the triangle between his legs.

He was wearing cotton slacks of some kind and I could smell his strong sweat through the thin fabric. I could see the bulge of his crotch pressing hard against the seams of his zipper.

He undid the pants and reached in to pull out his erection. The glans was already glistening with his viscous discharge. He grabbed my hair and roughly speared my mouth. I choked; he only pressed down harder. My bile blended with his seminal fluid as he thrust my head up and down the length of his cock.

He slapped my face with his free hand. It stung. He did it

again, and a hot pain spread over the right side of my head. Again. More pain. "Fucking whore!" he shouted at me. Another slap. "Fucking whore!"

Then the hand rested on my cheek where it had so recently struck me. At first it simply pressed against my injured flesh. Then it began to caress my face. His other hand released the tight grip on my hair and started to pet me with long tender motions. I kept my nose buried in the heavy pubic bush above Pedro's cock and began to control my gagging. I lost all consciousness of anything but the silky shaft that was in my mouth.

It was nearly hypnotic. It was wonderfully erotic. My cock was still hard and was still bobbing against me; I could feel a cool air on my asshole. My scrotum felt obscenely exposed.

It was the sound of Pedro's chest that brought me back to him. I had never heard the exact noise before. I thought at first that he was about to come. Then I realized he was crying. Little bits of sentences came through the quiet sobs. "Baby, I don't want…hurt you…sorry, baby…I don't…." His hands were both working, one still on my cheek, the other on the top of my head, still caressing and petting me.

His pelvis began almost indefinite thrusts. And soon he did come, sending waves of his thick stuff into me. With some of it still dribbling out the side of my mouth Pedro gently took me away from his cock and brought my head up to meet his. He kissed me and I could taste his cock and his mouth at the same time as his tongue pried open my lips.

I came while our mouths were opened to one another.

We never talked about the incident. For a while life went back to normal. A couple weeks later, though, there was another man, this time someone in a bar, who tried to pick me up. Again

Pedro attacked him viciously. Again, he took me back to his house and we repeated the ritual. It was precisely the same as the first time. I had never experienced anything quite as electric before in my life. Remembering the feel of the rug scraping against my knees and the exhibition I sensed I was giving as my scrotum was pressed between my thighs became two of the most important thoughts I would have while masturbating.

I only waited one week before I made it all happen again. It was entirely my responsibility this time. While Pedro wasn't looking, while we were sitting in someone's backyard, I surprised another of the guests with a sudden and unexpected kiss. He had barely had time to respond when Pedro was wrestling him to the ground and banging his head on the hard turf.

I don't remember making the other decisions consciously. They were hardly even decisions. I simply began to take more control of our sexuality. I didn't change any of it; I didn't want to. But I would be the first one to take off his clothes now. I would be the one who would see Pedro calmly watching television and I would go over and kneel between his legs. I would press my head into his crotch until he brought out his cock and let me suck it.

I no longer waited for Pedro to want to fuck me in bed, nor would I simply let him take any position he wanted. I would climb onto his belly and sit on his cock. I would ride it, lifting my ass up and setting it down with rapid motions as I watched the sex spread across his stomach up his chest and into his mind.

I was gradually becoming more and more exhilarated with my own passions. I wouldn't wait any longer for him to pull to the side of the road while he drove; I would spread across the car seat and unzip his fly while he drove up the highway. I would bang my head against the steering wheel while the car sped along.

None of this bothered Pedro at all. He seemed to love it. He seemed to match every bit of it. There was a rough edge that smoothed. There was more caressing, more kissing. There was also more ownership.

He began to be even more possessive and overtly proud of me. In a bar or at a party he would insist that every man there look at my ass and admire it. If he had a couple drinks he would even lower my pants and ignore my mock protests to show people just what it was he got in bed at night.

To my parents, he became more assertive. He gave up even the slightest niceties. He came to the house now and simply honked his car horn for me to run out and go away with him.

I hardly went home at all during August; I had moved in with him. There was my toothbrush in the bathroom and my responsibilities in the kitchen. The house money was in the cookie jar for me to do the shopping while he worked. He even had bought some clothes for me, underwear he had seen and admired in an ad. He thought it made my ass look more round.

If there was ever a moment when I felt ignored or worried about the approach of boredom I simply had to find a man who didn't understand and either I would approach him or allow him to approach me. I could always produce the explosion in Pedro I sought. I had begun to realize that it was not something he enjoyed; he barely understood it. But it would always happen.

At the end of the month I began to say things that made it clear I was going to return to college. Pedro was stunned. He became angry. He threatened me, then he began to plead.

If I was such a goddamn good student why couldn't I go to Brown? He'd pay my tuition if I went to Rhode Island State. There had to be a way to keep me from returning to that campus so many hundreds of miles away.

I refused to even consider the options. They were unreal to me. My parents, my professors, everything else in my life depended on the image of me at that school. I had to go. When he finally realized that I meant it, that he couldn't change this one thing about me, Pedro threw me out of the house. He gathered up all the clothes and all the mementos and drove me to my parents'. He wouldn't talk to me nor would he kiss me when we got there.

There was still another month before my classes began. Pedro shadowed me for the whole time. My mother and I would look out the kitchen window and see his car parked up the block. He would follow me to the supermarket, to the dentist, to the post office.

Sometimes at night I took my father's car and drove back to that bar in Providence. Whenever I did Pedro would be standing there in a corner watching me. If any man tried to talk to me, he would discover the big Portuguese tapping him on the back and asking for a word in private. I never discovered just what was said during those discussions, but the other man would always leave the bar quickly.

For years after that, whenever I would walk into a leather bar, I would only stay for one beer. I would look around at the men in their uniforms and their leather and listen to their conversations. I could never go home with them. They were all trying to look like and act like Portuguese truck drivers. I had already known the real thing; I wouldn't learn how to create something different for years to come.

It's been twenty years since I first crawled across the carpet in Pedro's living room. Every time I've told the story about that summer I've gotten different reactions. Some people comment on his "exploitation" of me, especially if I make myself sound like a victim. Others think he must have been a fool to have expected more from a teenager, if I make myself sound like a naive young boy. Almost everyone wants to believe I was somehow an injured party.

But when I'm honest with myself in the quiet moments I know that Pedro was the first man who ever loved me.

I have spent these twenty years living in ambiguity. The world changes, so do my roles and my perceptions of others. Men come and they go; love alters its images far too often.

There was a man, though, who loved me without limitation. Whatever else I think of him, I have to admit to myself that I am the one who left.

AN EDUCATION

After I finished college and did some graduate work I sought a job studying sex. I found a position in a small but prestigious operation in New York City and moved there to take the interesting, if low-paying, job as an editor. One of my duties was to attend various conferences, both to write about them and to represent the organization. I was especially useful when the director wanted to give a small but polite snub to another group. They couldn't really complain that they were being ignored if I was in attendance—I was officially an officer—but a kid in his twenties, the most junior member of the organization, was certainly not the one to lend prestige to whatever gathering was being held.

For the most part the meetings bored me. But there was finally one to be held in San Francisco, and the idea of going to that city and all the sexual possibilities that were supposed to be there made up for the too numerous treks to Baltimore and Buffalo that had been my fare.

To go on the trip I had to agree to stay with friends to help ease the cost—we were not a wealthy outfit by any means. I made the calls and other arrangements and went on my way.

I made the necessary appearance at the meeting, and performed the required social motions to the friends who were putting me up. Then, the first night possible, I went to Folsom Street.

There is probably no other one street whose image conjures up the intense sexuality of Folsom. Christopher and Santa Monica Boulevard have their own sexual connotations, but they don't instantly evoke visions of leather knights on steeds of black metal. Folsom does.

I found my way there and walked up and down, peering into the various bars and studying the explicit murals of sex that were on many of their walls. I had been to leather bars, of course. But I had, for whatever reason and with whatever help from the rest of the gay world, infused Folsom with a special intensity of expectation. The first places I went to didn't meet the standards I had created in my mind.

It wasn't till I got to the end of the strip of bars, to the last one whose address appeared on the special map a friend had given me, that I understood that this one night of the week belonged to just that one place. It was the night of the slave market.

As soon as I had opened the door and entered I knew that something special was going on. The crowd here outnumbered those of all the other places combined. It was packed with men, nearly all wearing leather, and the strong odor of the skin filled the air and sent an urgent excitement through my body.

I somehow moved through the loud boisterous crowd and got the attention of a bartender. With a cold bottle of beer firmly in my hand I moved towards the stage at the back of the room which was obviously the focus of everyone's attention. The night's show hadn't begun.

Between overheard conversations and quick readings of posters on the wall I got an idea of the action. Volunteers would be auctioned off to the highest bidder. The fee would be paid with scrip that had been accumulated by buying drinks at this bar during the week: for every beer a customer had received $5.00; for every drink of liquor he had gotten $10.00. It was obviously a popular event. Not only because there were so many people there, but because there was an active market in the play money. People were forming conglomerates in anticipation of the high prices their favorites would bring.

I was inexperienced in the fantasy world that this bar represented. While others around me were joking and teasing one another I was struck dumb with the concept of the selling and buying of men by men.

It was as though the most intense chimera had come true. Had I been older I would have understood it as a game or else I would have judged it strongly as inhuman. But at that moment in time its attraction was magnetic to me.

A master of ceremonies called for volunteers, a last chance to join the parade of nearly naked men that was lined up near the stage. My whole being wanted to march up there, but my feet wouldn't move.

When the moment passed I was torn between relief at having stayed in the audience and self-recrimination for not having walked into my private dreams.

The crowd was getting anxious. I was jostled often. I didn't resist, but tried to keep my place and my footing. I was sensing the leather and the masculine odors of the group and trying to be satisfied with those quick physical contacts and all-pervading smells as my consolation.

I don't know how long the one body stayed by my side. I became aware of it when the M.C. began his introduction to the program. The shoulder was pressed against mine; a thigh barely touched my hip. It was clothed in one of the leather jackets so common that night in that place. It was drinking beer. I didn't even dare to look at it.

The first man came on stage. He was wearing only a jock strap and a pair of black boots. Between his nipples was a chain. I had to study it for whole minutes before I realized that each end of the metal jewelry was attached to a small loop which was pierced through his skin. I felt a shudder seize my body; it was something between fear and excitement.

The bidding was fast and competitive. The sums seemed large; I didn't remember they were in play money denominations. The M.C. pulled on the chain and lifted the man's flesh up and away from his torso; his face registered a fierce sensation. It was finally over and a man ran to the stage to claim his prize.

The next man came on to the platform with a different demeanor and a different look. He was as cocky as the first had been submissive. He, too, had the same jock; but he also wore leather chaps and boots. His muscles were prominent.

The bidding was repeated. The man who won the auction was as anxious for his prize as the first had been, but when he arrived at the stage he didn't take hold of his purchase, he leaned over and smilingly fondled the man's boots.

The body next to me spoke. "Which do you want to be? The top or the bottom?"

I just shrugged, not daring to commit myself. His hand grazed over my ass, but I thought I should just ignore its touch. When it came to rest there, I didn't know how to tell him to remove it, or whether I wanted him to.

We stood and watched the rest of the show. The men kept appearing on the platform; they would display themselves and offer themselves up to the humiliation of the M.C.'s banter. The hand on my ass left only to retrieve beers for both of us. It would always return.

As the evening progressed the hand ended its passivity. It began to knead my buttocks, first carefully, then with more power. It sought out the cleft between my cheeks and pressed hard, leaving my underwear sticking in the wet crack. I still hadn't dared to talk to its owner.

When the last man had been sold I had no defense to keep me from facing my companion. I turned and looked in his face. He was attractive in a way; his expression was emotionless. It seemed as though he were simply studying me.

We talked a little. I told him I had never been to that bar before. He explained the weekly auction, filling in those details I hadn't picked up earlier. "Anyone can be a volunteer. For any role." I blushed.

We had more beer and the crowd thinned out a little. I knew instinctively that his conversation was testing me. I had few pieces of vocabulary to convey my interest. It was just my being there that kept him intrigued. I obviously wasn't going to run.

Nor did I struggle when he would put his hand on the back of my neck and roughly massage me while he spoke. I didn't move when that same hand went back to my ass. Nor did I flinch when it came to my chest and unbuttoned my shirt. It went underneath the fabric and searched for my nipples; it felt my stomach. It must have been satisfied. He didn't leave.

My mind was remembering every story I had ever read and every fantasy I had ever had. The truth was that most of my sexuality had been outside the boundaries that included this bar and this man. Yet I had come here and I had defined myself as belonging here. It was only difficult because I did not yet know the words and the rites that took place in this arena. I thought of pain but could only sense arousal.

At some certain point he looked at me in a way that I knew was announcing some significant statement. "I gotta piss. The john's too crowded. Wanna come to the alleyway with me?"

I nodded.

I walked out and the sound of Folsom Street's traffic seemed serene after the loud music of the bar. We walked only a short distance. My cock was hard; it made it difficult to move my legs. We got to an alley and I followed him in. He stood facing me. He unzipped his fly and brought out his cock. It hung in a soft arc out from his body. He waited.

I had never done this. I knew I didn't have to, and I knew I wanted to. I went to my knees and accepted the half-soft flesh into my mouth. His belly contracted and soon a gush of warm urine came into my mouth. I was split by two different levels of experience: I thought that it didn't taste nearly as bad as I had imagined, and I also felt myself as a supplicant before a priest.

When he was done he stayed as he had been, his cock in my mouth. A hand rested against my neck and forbade me to move. His cock grew hard and large. He slowly began to move it in and out of my mouth. He was extremely gentle, as though he had sensed my inexperience. I stayed as I was and felt honored to have this flesh inside me. I closed my eyes and imagined that he had chosen me from those who had been on the stage, that he had bound my hands and he had brought me to this place to claim his due. Just as I was imagining the words that had brought me to my knees in my dream, his cock splashed his hot fluid inside me.

He took me back into the bar. The acts in the alley had changed all that went between us. I was now told where to stand. I was interrogated; the mutual conversation ended. I was explored by his hands, no longer simply tested. When he told me he was taking me home to his house it only seemed right.

We slept soundly. In the morning he fucked me from behind with his arms wrapped tightly around my chest. We showered and I automatically took the towel to dry his body. He seemed to expect it when it happened. We went into the kitchen and I was surprised to find another man there.

While the two of us had put on our clothes, this new person was sitting naked at the table drinking coffee. He greeted the other man with a smile; he was obviously happy. He ignored me but excitedly stood to show the other wide bands of black and blue that striped his buttocks. Then he presented the front of his body and the rough scabs that had gathered over his nipples.

He was overtly proud of himself and described his own adventures of the last night with intimate detail. I was already hard again as I listened to him even though I had just orgasmed not an hour earlier while I had been fucked.

There was a moment's tension. The man I had already known was angry. I suppose it was jealousy though I was too inexperienced to recognize it. The other man jested and kissed him to calm his feelings.

We three drank coffee. Their conversation drifted into domestic details; they evidently were sharing this small house. As they talked I tried not to be too plain in my study of the new man's body. He was blond, with almost no hair on his flesh except on his head, a growth around his open crotch and little tufts that showed from under his armpits. The nakedness of his flesh made the red scabs around his nipples even more distinct. I coveted them greatly.

They turned their attention to me. They both asked much more mundane questions about me and my life than he had the night before. I explained I was staying with friends. They took it for granted that I would now move in with them.

I didn't argue. We arranged for the man I had met to go with me to collect my clothes. I detailed my schedule for the conference and, when they insisted, defined which events I had to attend and which I could avoid.

While we walked up and down the hills of San Francisco I finally had to admit that the man had never told me his name. I felt strange that I was going to move into his home without knowing it.

He laughed. "Brad."

We got the bags and I left a short note. At Brad's house we deposited my belongings, then went over to Castro Street and sat in the window table of a restaurant and I watched as the parade of men marched past me. I talked about the excitement of this army of homosexuals, the lusty reaction to their well-developed chests and their curving asses. Brad simply said, "You get over it after you've lived here a while."

I went back to the conference that afternoon. Most of the sessions were set up in the same way: there was a speaker, then a panel would react. There were occasional group discussions, but the panel was the main format being used. Most were held in a large auditorium downtown. It was set up as a lecture hall with the seats in rows, each row higher than the first. One could sit in the last and look down at the group as though from the balcony of a large theater.

The presentations were boring; the people were uninspired. The participants seemed pale compared to Brad and the one other man whose name I still didn't know. I escaped back to their house near Folsom Street as soon as I thought my obligations would allow.

The two men were both there. The other one, still naked, gave me a small greeting. When I found Brad he was sitting on a chair on a little terrace overlooking a backyard. He accepted a kiss. "Take off your clothes, get some sun."

I declined. He frowned. "Take off your clothes." The sun was obviously a ruse. He wanted me nude as the other man was. I stripped and sat beside him; he was much more pleasant once it had been accomplished.

As the late afternoon slipped away and as the three of us ate dinner the other man had cooked I began to understand the implicit rules of the house. We two were always to be naked. More, we were always to be ready to have sex. Without clothing to hide us Brad could see whenever either of us had an erection or the beginning of one.

I was the first. It had begun while the sun was still shining on us. It was erotic just to be outdoors unclothed. I had barely felt the blood enter my cock. But I heard Brad call out to the other man. The blond arrived and smiled; he knelt beside me and took my cock in his mouth. The warm sucking was indescribably wonderful. But it was nowhere near as exciting as the touch of Brad's hard hands as they came and played with my nipples, both at the same time. I shot quickly and intensely.

I didn't really have the courage to ask about the speedy and seemingly impersonal act. As soon as I had come the blond had stood and, after a brief smile, returned to the kitchen. Brad continued a conversation about California history just where it had been interrupted.

At the dinner table the blond was the one whose erection caught Brad's attention. At Brad's insistence he was telling his tales about last night with even more detail. He had gone home with a man he had met at another bar and had been lashed to the beam of a cellar playroom where the man had beaten him with a leather strap. The recollection of the adventure excited the blond.

Brad suggested the blond fuck me. It was said easily, but I knew any hesitation would have been followed by an order as direct as that to strip earlier. I didn't know how to proceed, though I had immediately decided to comply. The blond had risen up and retrieved a jar of lubricant. He greased his now-hard cock lewdly in front of me, and told me to get to the floor on my hands and knees. I did.

He moved into my ass slowly. There was hardly any pain even though his cock was substantial. I had never been fucked in this position, certainly not on the kitchen floor. It was deeply exciting, but not passionately so. There was some other kind of eroticism to this easy and matter-of-fact sex. Even when Brad came over to me and brought out his own hard cock for me to suck while the blond continued to thrust inside me I found myself and my feelings relaxing into an acceptance of their lust and not trying to match it.

They both came with loud shouts and groans and I was able to feel, for one quick moment, both their cocks pulsing at the same time.

When it was done and we had each washed a little bit we went back to the table.

The blond and I each achieved another erection that night. Mine came while I was spread out on the couch. Brad was watching television; it was the explorations of his fingers against my balls that caused me to harden. When he called the blond this time he suggested that it was time for me to fuck. I started to get up but Brad held my shoulders tight. The blond greased my cock and straddled my midsection, then carefully lowered his ass onto me and moved himself up and down my erection until my stomach spasmed my fluids into him.

The fucking made him hard. He simply slipped my cock out of him and brought his own up to my mouth. Brad's hands unnecessarily opened my jaws and let the blond move in and out of me with slow drives that would just barely force me to gag at their deepest penetration. Brad's palm felt my throat as I swallowed the blond's cum when he finally orgasmed.

That night—and the rest of the nights for the rest of my stay—we three slept in the same bed. I was in the middle. Brad would fuck me, usually in the morning. If he felt my cock hard he would maneuver the blond's mouth or ass onto it; he would have me reciprocate whenever the blond was erect.

The easy and total sexual domination towered over my dreams. More than I could possibly have foreseen, those days and nights at that house were the fulfillment of my fantasies.

Toward the end of the week I stayed with them I found Brad reading the program of my conference. I had almost totally ended my participation and hadn't paid attention to the schedule in days.

He suddenly burst into laughter. "A panel on S&M?! They're going to have a panel on S&M!" He asked if I could bring guests. I assured him there was no security in any event.

Brad called the blond in and announced that the three of us were going to attend the session that afternoon. He told the blond to dress. "Dress way up," he ordered.

That afternoon I found myself walking through downtown San Francisco with two men clothed entirely in black leather. Each had matching chaps over his jeans, heavy boots on his feet, a leather shirt underneath a leather jacket and a leather cap on his head. The blond wore a steel chain around his neck with an oversized padlock in the front. They both had handcuffs and keys hanging from their belts. Brad's were on the left; the blond's on the right.

The academics who were gathered watched wordlessly as the three of us climbed to the last two tiers of seats. At Brad's instruction the blond and I sat directly in front of him.

The speaker, a psychologist who often dominated these events, gave a talk. I often had to translate the academic terms for my two companions. After the brief speech there was a panel discussion as usual. The five people were, as always, liberal in their views; it was a year when being nonjudgmental was in vogue.

As soon as they had begun their discussion, Brad had lifted his legs and placed one boot on one of my shoulders and the other on one of the blond's. The blond smiled and rubbed his face against the surface. Then, with long, long theatrical motions, he began to lick the leather. I hesitated only for the moment it took for Brad's hand to grip my neck, then I also began to mouth my boot.

The two hundred or so people who had assembled for the presentation started to grow restless. Their bodies were noticeably squirming. One by one they would look over their shoulders at the three of us in the back rows. The panel continued its discussion.

Brad took back the boots. He leaned over and a hand snaked around each of us. He deftly unbuttoned my shirt and the blond's. He pulled them both out of the restraint of our belts and spread them open to expose our chests. Each of his hands took hold of one of our nipples and he began to twist and dig. He had never, for the times he played with my chest, hurt so badly. I had no choice but to start to writhe in my seat. The glancing touches of the blond's body told me he was being forced to do the same.

I looked over at my partner and saw that his mouth was moving against the offending hand. It was not the gentle touch that lips usually gave to Brad's body but an anxious, almost desperate plea. I followed his example, hoping that my mouth could gain my body some relief. Neither of us, though, tried to escape.

The crowd was now in turmoil. The panel discussion must have been continuing; there were words coming through the loudspeaker. But the audience was paying more attention to the three of us than to the program.

Brad finally, thankfully stopped and both the blond and

I sank into repose. I turned back to look at Brad after I had recovered from the assault. He was looking straight at the panel with a broad grin on his face.

The blond and I rebuttoned our shirts. We stuffed them back into our pants. The three of us got up and left the room.

Back at their apartment Brad was in a state of high agitation. Even if I hadn't been able to sense it I could have known something out of the ordinary was going to happen by the expression of anxious curiosity that was on the blond's face.

We two stripped and Brad led us into the bedroom. He laid our bodies out on the bed. He brought out rope and fastened my wrists to the blond's ankles; then did the same with my legs and the blond's arms. Our faces were forced into each other's crotch. We were both hard. We both sucked in the other's erection. Brad's belt landed in loud and painful blows on my ass and then on the other's. When I thought I had been taken to the limit of my endurance Brad got undressed. His own cock was erect and he quickly greased it. He fucked me with great violence, but with so much intensity that he came quickly.

I went back to the conference the next day. I was greeted at the door by one of the organizers who politely informed me that it would be better if I stopped coming to the sessions. He couldn't seem to look me in the eye as he explained that I was making the other participants uneasy.

I was very, very pleased.

TRANSITIONS

It is hard to find the ways that people have altered my life. The giving that I have received and that which I've offered which combined to produce who I am and who people around me have become is usually too difficult to define concretely.

But a part of me is easily shown to be the accumulation of the effects of certain men. When I dress for sex I can see who has given me myself when I look in the mirror. The boots were chosen by Jim; the chaps declared necessary by John; Garry asked for the reflecting sunglasses; Tom was the first to admire the jock strap hidden beneath the jeans that Steve insisted I wear; Jason adored the uniform shirt. It's insufficient to claim these are superficial items. They represented many things to many men. They have become a reflection of who I might be....

I was walking home across the city from a trick's house on a warm sunny day in San Francisco. He had been attractive and horny. I had his name and number on a slip of paper in my pocket and I thought it might be one that would be used.

I stopped at a red light. In front of me, at the head of the traffic waiting to cross the intersection, was a man sitting astride a motorcycle. Even in the heat of the summer day he wore a full leather outfit; a black metal helmet, leather pants, boots, and a jacket opened to reveal a hairy chest. He was staring at me.

I had taken off my shirt. I had never had a developed body but I was only in my late twenties and my natural torso was enough to attract attention. I smiled at his obvious interest. The lights changed and I walked to the other corner and made my way up Divisadero.

Traffic sounds surrounded me. I paid no attention to the roar of the motorcycle until it had jumped up onto the sidewalk. He stopped it only a few feet in front of me. There was no escape from talking to him; he blocked my path. I didn't want to escape anyway.

We introduced ourselves; he lived close to me. He had an appointment now; what was I doing later in the afternoon? A glass of wine at his place? Sure.

I went back to my apartment and laughingly told my roommate about the black knight who had so boldly propositioned me. "You aren't going over there, are you?" "Why not?" "Leather?" "Why not?"

I knocked on his door at just the hour we had agreed upon. He was obviously pleased to see me. I followed him up to the second floor flat. He did pour the wine; I refused the offer of dope.

He still wore the leather pants. He was older than I had thought that afternoon, well into his forties. He was attractive, though not handsome. He was masculine, but not intensely so.

I nearly smiled when he awkwardly announced that his sexual interests were S&M—that had been clear to me. He quickly added that he didn't have to have heavy sex. Did I just want to stay in his apartment and fuck?

What was the option to his apartment? I was puzzled.

There was a special room in the basement, he explained.

I wanted to go there.

He altered his mood then. He needed a transition, and he stood and came over to me. My cock was hard in my Levis. One of his hands rested on my head while his other reached around to a back pocket. I saw a pair of metal handcuffs as he put them on the small table beside me. He quickly removed my shirt, then took the handcuffs and secured my wrists behind my back.

He led me down the back stairs. A cool breeze flowed over naked skin and made my cock drip with the image I had in my mind just then. Half nude, bound, being taken to a black room by an unknown man. I was a slave, a captive to be used by this man at his will.

He unlocked a door and reached in to turn on a light. He left me at the entrance while he went about switching on other subtle lamps and finally a stereo. Religious music, deep chants sung with masculine voices, overtook the room. I was brought inside. A plain wooden platform sat in the center. At each corner chains connected it to the ceiling and the floor. He took my body and spread it stomach-down on the wood, then unlocked the handcuffs.

He put leather restraints on each of my wrists and ankles, then took metal clamps and, having removed the handcuffs, he secured each of my limbs to a chain. Somehow the ends of the table disassembled. I was left with only my belly on the wood. My arms and legs were being held only by the bondage of the chains.

He put a hand on my ass and began slapping it. It wasn't a choreographed spanking, but each slap increased with intensity. I responded by lifting myself up to receive his blows.

He went to the wall and reached for a leather strap. There were dozens of belts, paddles, crops and whips on display; I was both relieved and disappointed that he chose one of the least foreboding.

He used the strap on my ass. The blows were easy—the real pain came from the accumulation of their effect. The sensations became intense and hurtful. He paused. I waited for more, but they didn't come.

Instead he moved till his body was in front of me, unzipped his pants and took out his cock. While I mouthed his erection he played hard with my nipples. They were exposed by the absence of a part of the platform and I could smell the leather chaps that decorated his body. I was intensely excited by his fucking my mouth with thrusting motions. His cock was unfortunately easy to suck—I wished it had been longer to make me gag. It just slid in and out of my lips without giving me any sensation of pain.

I was rubbing the tip of my own erection against the wooden platform that held my midsection. I came with a great shudder just as the strange taste of his cum filled my mouth.

I was waiting for more. There wasn't any. He released me from the bondage and gave back my clothes; we returned to the upstairs apartment where he poured more wine and told me about his life. I wished he'd sent me home with no information, just an order to reappear the next day.

He hesitated at one point, obviously about to make a statement he wanted me to pay attention to. "You know, I do that for money. Sometimes people want a third person there. Would you be interested?"

I was, of course. I told him there had been times as a teenager when men would assume that I expected to be paid. I had found it erotic. Besides, I was out of work. Why not, for a few dollars?

He became very businesslike, telling me exactly how much he would receive and how much of that I would get. He asked what clothes I had to present the image that his customers would respond to—they were all men interested in playing in his black room.

All I had were heavy boots and a leather vest. "That's enough. Just wear those and your jeans. No shirt. They'll like that."

He told me he'd call when there was a man who wanted both of us. I went home then, slightly dissatisfied with him but intensely intrigued with the idea of being paid for sex. My roommate was incredulous. "How could you?" "Easily."

The phone rang the next day: someone would be at his apartment that afternoon. I was to go to the back of the building and stand by the door we had entered, wearing only the vest, no shirt.

I walked through the neighborhood with my chest bare and the vest smelling. My jeans were tight; the boots were scuffed. Men who had seen me every day for a year noticed me for the first time as I passed them.

I waited where I had been told to stand and soon I heard the two of them coming down the stairs. The entrance to the black room wasn't visible from any apartment nor from the street; there was total privacy even though the stairway was out of doors. The man I knew was dressed in the same full leather he had worn the day I had met him, though now a leather cap was on his head rather than a helmet. Behind him, moving very slowly and cautiously, was a man naked except for a leather hood. It blocked off all his vision as well as his ability to speak. Only slits for breathing were cut into it at his nostrils.

A chain ran from one of his nipples to the other. Clamps secured the chain to his tits. From the center of the chain came another line of linked steel which the leatherman was using to guide the utterly helpless figure.

The man went through the ritual of turning on the lights and music. With silent motions he indicated when he wanted help with his efforts.

We soon had the new man spread-eagled on the same platform I had been attached to. The end slats of wood were again released and I knew the sensation of being suspended that the figure felt. Only a small part of the platform remained in place to support him. This, I realized, was the way I had looked. Totally vulnerable and open.

This man wanted more in his reality than I had allowed myself in my fantasies. He received a beating with the most vicious looking items on the walls. Bright red stripes soon lined his back and ass. His body writhed with brutal reactions.

Somehow a private signal passed between the tortured man and the leatherman who was inflicting so much pain. The leatherman stopped his beating and ran his hands over the flesh he had just so recently whipped. He nodded to me to do the same. I felt the heat where the lashes and paddles had landed. I saw the crisscross of lines where the crop had cut.

The hood was removed. The supplicant figure kissed the hands that had just attacked him. I was nodded to stand in front of the bound man, and the leatherman and I both removed hard cocks from our pants at the same time. As my erection went into the mouth the other fucked the ass.

The two of us eyed one another as we pumped. The leatherman's hands came to my chest and twisted my nipples. We both shot quickly.

The man was released. He was delighted. He handed a wad of bills to the leatherman, then the three of us sat and drank beer. The man asked me many questions and complimented me on my appearance and my actions. When he left he playfully knelt and kissed my boots. The playfulness, though, had an edge of sincerity. After he left I drank another beer and pondered my astonishment: that man's submission had been as erotic to me as my own had been.

We had many more sessions over the next few weeks. I didn't really understand then the extent the leatherman went to to arrange for my participation in them. Still each encounter fascinated me: I soon learned how to administer the beatings myself. I was taught all the words and orders and symbols. When the leatherman would go off for a day at the beach or to lunch with a friend he would let me stay in his apartment and answer the phone that clients used to secure his services.

I was actually often asked to join him at the shore or at the restaurants. He wanted to introduce me to his friends. I had my own friends though, and was more interested in the men who would call for sex and fantasy.

I had started to go to leather bars by myself, wearing my vest with no shirt. The legions of men who would play with my nipples and take me to alleyways behind Folsom Street were exciting to me. Watching the men who would kneel in front of me for the sake of paying me money still excited me as much.

The leatherman eventually became very angry. I had used him; I had come into his life just to learn his tricks and just to be taught his profession. What was so very wrong with that, I asked. And didn't he remember that everything that happened was his idea?

He asked me to become his lover. Once he made the admission of that desire his emotions could be seen more coherently. Lovers don't come to life in this fantasy, I said. They must, he replied. He looked suddenly very old and very sad.

When I went to Folsom Street I began to more often be the one who sought out other men's nipples and who led them into the alleyways. The men who would call and hire me showed me new techniques. I became increasingly competent. My reputation grew.

I was soon living luxuriously. As many as five men a day would come to my new apartment—I no longer needed a roommate to split the rent—and I would use any of a number of newly acquired instruments on their bodies and my new power on their minds.

Some men took me on trips to distant cities. Others would travel absurd miles to be with me for just the hour their money would pay for. I ate in fine restaurants. Many of the men who had hired the two of us now came to me. Even though I never had an elaborate black room like the leatherman's I did have more than enough to create their fantasies.

Soon I had a whole wardrobe of leather. Chaps, pants, shirts and vests all hung in my closet. The clothes were to lure men into alleyways or to provide others with expensive entertainment. The money seemed unreal: it was just paper that had accumulated in my pocket and crowded my wallet if I didn't spend it.

I joined a group of other men who would sit in the bars and restaurants of Castro Street early in the day. We would regather very late at night in the taverns on Folsom Street. We all knew where we had been in the hours between.

We began to recognize one another. We'd nod as our proud bodies walked the side streets of San Francisco; we'd smile knowingly as we passed in the corridors of the best hotels. There was only one reason for a leatherboy to be in the Huntington at three in the afternoon.

We couldn't really talk to one another, it wasn't part of the life. If one lusted for me he would call me and tell me about some strange and exotic trick who wanted a three-way. But, of course, the one who called would have to test the goods first and make sure they met the requirements. His own reputation was on the line, you see.

I would allow the deception. One by one they would come to my apartment with their big cocks and their massive chests. Tired from their roles, they would relax. They would ask me to put on my leather and then they would kneel in front of me and suck me hard, then they would lick the chaps and nuzzle my sweaty balls.

There was never a customer, of course. But they could never admit that to me, perhaps not even to themselves.

Time ceased to have meaning. A day was a day; there were no weekends. There was no reason not to have a beer with lunch. There was no pressure to call a friend. There would always be some businessman from Des Moines who was desperate to discover the secrets of life in San Francisco.

The fantasies began to blur with one another. I would sometimes forget that I was supposed to be a policeman and would start to give a drill instructor's orders. I would spend the whole hour and overlook the expectation that it would end with my cock up a customer's ass.

I floated through two years with the money and the fantasies and the strange reality of life in California. Finally I thought I might drown. I gave up the apartment, sold my furniture and bought a ticket back to the East.

I did not give up everything I had learned. I kept my leather. I would bring it out and wear it on cool nights in Chelsea. I watched the hungry eyes that followed me from bar to bar; I would sometimes let the tentative hands touch me. I would smile when some embarrassed businessman recognized me on the street, anxious because I had left my place and hadn't stayed at the end of a telephone number in San Francisco.

The leatherman followed my progress. He had kept wanting me to love him while I sold my body to wanderers with false names. I had refused. He was furious when I left California and now he called me across the continent and wanted to know how I could have left him. I told him I had never been there to leave.

There was still a lot of sex, but now the men would repeat. They would visit me often, not just once. They would stay a while afterwards and drink tea and talk. It became a relief to learn the intimacies of their bodies and their persons.

I loved them. I would fondle their asses and cup their cock and balls and I would kiss their lips. Each one became an adventure. Every time one returned I would renew my explorations and discover something new about him.

When a man would go too far away from me I would get upset and often leave him. I would tie his hands if he asked, and would slap his face if he wanted that experience. But I was not, I would have to tell him, a policeman or a drill instructor. When one would try to thank me with a gift I would become suspicious and often I'd leave him and never see him again.

I would not humiliate them. Not one, not once. How could I call you a pig or a slut or a cunt or anything less than a man? I had chosen you, I'd explain; if you are less than desirable, I'm the one who's made the worst statement about himself.

I still used some things I had learned. There is a certain way to tie a knot or use a belt or talk while a man is sucking your cock. Those things remained.

The leatherman kept calling. I would tell him what was happening and he would be jealous. Why wasn't he the one who received these pleasures, he'd asked. Wasn't he the one who started it all? Why wasn't he the one with me now?

I couldn't answer him.

AN HOUR'S STOPOVER

It began in Rustler's in Boston. I didn't have many expectations for the weeknight visit to the city, mostly I was just wasting time. I hoped I might find a trick, but mainly I was killing the night while a friend from Portland had his fun with someone else on Beacon Hill. All I really thought would happen was I'd have a few beers here and then I'd sneak back into the apartment and sleep on the couch. My Portland friend and I would drive back to Maine the next morning.

Leather bars in Boston don't thrill me. They seem to be full of guilt-ridden Roman Catholics and college students too young to know what the scene is all about. I don't think I'd mind even then, but Bostonians, as a group, are all so pretentious about everything. They think they know it all.

Only a beer or so into the night and a group of laughing kids came into the bar. They smelled of BU and Northeastern and any one of a dozen other campuses in the city. I had had my eye on a hot-looking little fucker in one corner and another, slightly older man standing against the far wall. Mainly I had been interested in playing the cruising game with those two. Maine doesn't give me many opportunities to practice the subtle mating movements that urban gays have taken to a new level of art. It had been fun to watch each of the two men as their strategies for my seduction had begun to emerge.

But soon there was some motion. A tall guy left the college group and walked toward my corner of the room. A baseball cap on his head contradicted the leather jacket he wore. He walked right up and said a quick "Hi." "Hello," I replied. He was taller than me, something I'm not used to. My 6'1" is usually enough to hold a height advantage. He had a quick, nice voice with a deep tone. I actually wondered if it had been professionally trained.

He spilled it out quickly: Had I been cruising him? Well…yes, I had noticed him in the group. I didn't admit that I couldn't make out his features when he had been standing across the room in the shadows and that I had basically just been noticing the bunch of them as they walked in. His chatter picked up. God, he sounded young. There was a giggle between words, a sly, almost cynical nature about him. Youth doesn't know enough to take some things seriously.

"What do you do?" he asked after we had exchanged names.

"I'm a writer and a photographer."

"Jesus, I'm so tired about hearing about writers and photographers. I mean, what do you do for a living?"

Little snot. "I am a writer and a photographer…for a living."

He hesitated. "Where do you live?"

"Portland, Maine."

A little hiss came from his throat. "Do you know what that

does for your credibility? A writer from Maine, for Christ's sake."

For a split second I stood there caught between a desire to slap his face, an intuition to walk away and an impulse to laugh out loud at him.

Finally, I said: "There's a scene in *Rich and Famous* where the Jacqueline Bisset character talks about the arrogance of youth. You're one of the best examples I ever met."

He didn't like the analogy. His back stiffened a bit and it took a while for the smile to return. Okay, he asked, what did I write? I told him: features for a Portland newspaper, porn, commentary for gay magazines. I write what I can get paid for and then, when I have the chance, I write what I want to. He was intrigued now. Anything he's heard of? "What do you read?" He named a few periodicals. I had written for a couple of them so I listed the titles of some articles and stories. The whole exchange altered its complexion. He begrudgingly admitted admiring some of my writing; his admiration was directed toward the heaviest S&M pieces.

I had shifted my physical stance by then. I'll give him one thing, his body answered each of my moves. Thigh moved closer to thigh, arm to arm, leather grazed wool and jeans brushed against jeans. The conversation continued.

We both seemed to be asking each other: What's going on? The realities quickly slipped in: He had a lover, I had no place to take anyone. I quashed a momentary impulse to rent a motel room. No, too much to put out for a still unknown quantity.

His story started to flesh out as he talked more. The lover—his second or third since his teens—worked during the day. A strict nine-to-five existence. At night they were monogamous, but those nine-to-five hours were play time for my new little friend. We stopped talking. During the moment's hesitation I could sense each of us thinking about trying our luck elsewhere. No. We each silently decided to keep on. It's strange when you know that the connection with someone has gone past the usual bar trip. No matter what else was happening, I could sense the two of us pass a threshold.

We started to talk dirty. Nothing heavy, just an exchange of physical compliments. I was constantly aware that he was young—twenty-three, he said. My thirty-five years were about to turn over for thirty-six. Not so much, but it felt like there was an entire generation between us. Our hands began to roam subtly over each other's body. Ever so slightly I tested him with a palm on his ass. He shifted to give me more access to his buttocks.

The conversation was frustrating me. He laughed at every statement; every time there was a seriousness in our words, he cut through it with that giggle. I flashed back:

> It is fifteen years ago. I am younger than he is today. I am in New York. I am dating a man in his thirties. Handsome and articulate as I only dream of becoming. He is a "success," "famous." After our first meeting at a party, he takes me home with him and we drink cognac on his terrace overlooking the Hudson. The next morning, after sex more practiced than I'm used to, he hands me a copy of one of his record albums. Later, he takes me to plays his friends have written or produced or acted

in and to restaurants I had only read about. His body is beautiful and more open to my touch than anyone else's has ever been before. But we both know I am too young. I am too inexperienced to know when and how to be appreciative. I boast about this man with all my friends after each time I see him, but when I'm with him I laugh, blush, don't articulate the depth of emotion that's going through me. Finally one night—one night that's been full of magic—we are in bed. He is teaching me how to have sex. The blow jobs I'm used to giving and receiving won't do for him; he wants hands to roam and mouths to eat and asses to be stuffed with professional dignity. I giggle. He becomes more and more angry. He makes moves I'm so desperate to receive that I can't react. He's about to fuck me while his mouth licks first one nipple and then the next. The sensation is so overwhelming that I can't control myself. My only defense is to laugh again. He pulls away and rolls off my body. "Get out!" His voice is hard and harsh. I don't even know enough to be able to apologize or to cry. As I put my clothes on it is his eyes that spill the tears. I won't let mine out for another five years. I am too young.

Is this boy/man doing the same thing to me? He has read my work and knows I am serious. He has the words to honor me, but his adolescent discomfort won't leave the words alone. He had to snicker through them. When I began to get angry he at least did know enough to back off. He became a different kind of insolent. He argued. He certainly was old enough to act like an adult, he insisted, he certainly was mature enough to know what's going on in life.

Ah, the arrogance of youth!

We talked more seriously. I was surprised: he took the criticism I threw at him and didn't walk away. It dawned on me that he was upset that I, personally, thought about him in those ways. He wanted to prove something to me: that he was a man, I supposed. Well, I had to acknowledge my pleasure that he at least had chosen me to prove himself to.

There was a strong sexual connection between us. It was enough to send stirrings to my crotch. I wanted him—badly. I suddenly touched a prick of insecurity inside me. I was aware of his attractiveness. His face seemed more than occasionally handsome in the dim bar light. The body hidden under the coat and jeans looked lithe and athletic. Did he want me in the same way? The years I have don't frighten me, but they weigh. I had never noticed my twenties go by, but each year of my thirties has been a moment marked in my consciousness. None of those years felt badly—on the contrary, I love the sense of age, maturity and competence that grew with them. But I don't trust their attractiveness to youth in Boston. In Portland the whole thing is different. There are fewer men and they treat each other more carefully. In New York, age is desirable. But here in Boston the trip is sharply defined: the boys lust after each other and the men look on hungrily.

But there wasn't much doubt he did want me. We talked

about S&M and he asked me if I was a top. What did I do in a scene? I decided to play with his mind: I looked into his eyes and said, "I'm heavy...*very* heavy." He smiled—wrong move, kid—"I like that," he said. "I am too. I'd love to be a bottom for you. But I'd want to top you besides."

"Never."

He was suddenly furious, no smile now, "Why not?"

"I wouldn't trust you to know how to do it. You're too young."

"I'm good at it. People tell me that all the time."

"Not good enough for me. With me—you're on the bottom."

"That's not fair."

"Life's not fair."

"Bastard."

"Arrogant youth."

He became *very* angry then. I had a hard on.

I wondered if his muscles were twitching so hard because he wanted to stomp away. "You shouldn't judge people by superficial standards. You don't know that I'm not a good top just because I'm only twenty-three. I am a *very* good top."

I hesitated. Usually I wouldn't bother to respond to a statement like that. I don't like explaining S&M. I must have already been caught though. "You might be. I just doubt it. You'd have to prove it to me, you'd have to prove it a great deal before I ever went bottom for you. Look, don't get me wrong, I don't mind sucking a cock, I love it. I'm not going to lie to you and tell you I never get fucked. I'm not being an asshole about it. I'm just telling you that it doesn't happen often and it doesn't happen at all with guys as much younger than myself as you are. It's just not in the books."

We shifted to a softer conversation after a calming silence. Then we began to kiss. They were wide open, tongue-exploring kisses, intense and demanding. I could feel his hard on as our groins rubbed against each other. He put his arms around me and acted the aggressor. There was an enthusiasm about him, a lack of hesitancy, that only added to my image of his youthfulness. We whispered more dirty talk between embraces.

I broke it off to go to the john. He followed me in a few moments later, just as I was shaking my cock dry. He looked at it. "I want to drink your piss." "Sometime," I promised. I thought the whole idea of a piss scene was turning him on so I lingered while he stood at the urinal. Finally he blushed, "I only came in to watch you. I don't really have to do it myself; even if I did, I couldn't while you're standing here." His shyness was strangely endearing.

We went back to the main room of the bar, got more beer and started up again. "I want to drink your piss," he repeated. "I want to beat your ass," I insisted. We kept up the embraces and battering of each other's erections until the lights came up to announce closing time. The idea of a motel cropped up in my mind again. No, not now. I got paper and pen from the bartender and wrote out my name and phone number. I gave it to him, but pointedly did not ask for his in return. It would have to be his decision. That's partially an ethic of mine about people with lovers, but it was also part of the trip I was playing out: The youth should call the man.

When I told my Portland friend about the encounter during the drive back to Maine I discovered myself telling him that the whole dynamic had been somehow more satisfying than most of the actual tricks I had had in Boston. There was just something sensuously delightful in the entire exchange. "Will he call you? Would he actually drive to Maine just to fuck with you?" "I don't know. We'll see."

He didn't call for well over a week. I was packing for a holiday vacation and he flashed through my mind. I decided he had chickened out. But just as I was leaving the apartment the phone did ring. It was he. We went through some friendly banter. I explained I was on my way to Boston to spend the night with some friends, then on to New York. He was wonderfully seductive on the phone; he knew how to work that voice of his. He told me he had just wanted to make contact. I had an image of him cleaning out his wallet and leafing through the trick cards to sift out the ones that were worth keeping and to decide which others to throw away.

"I might have some time tomorrow, on my way to New York. Will you be home?" Yes. "I'll call you." I finally accepted his phone number.

I drove down to the suburb of Medford where I was spending the night. The two men I was visiting had prepared a lavish dinner; we sat around with drinks and talked about writing and publishing and careers late into the night.

The next morning I woke and showered. I remembered the youth. I wasn't conscious of hiding my purpose from my hosts until I found myself acutely embarrassed when Laurence walked into the room while I was on the phone. I was listening to the boy/man tell me it wouldn't work, there were workmen in his apartment repairing the ceiling. Laurence raised an eyebrow when I had hung up, obviously aware of the content of the call from the one side of the conversation he had heard.

"Do you really believe *that?*" he asked. "Why shouldn't I?" I answered, though it sounded weak even to me.

He stuck in my mind throughout the trip to New York. On the day I was scheduled to return to Maine I got up two hours earlier than necessary and packed the car to give myself a chance to spend the afternoon with him—if he wanted to spend the afternoon with me. But I drove directly into a traffic jam and immediately lost the extra time.

It's easy to just trick with someone. Just meet them, go home, fuck and say good-bye. The next time you see the person it's just a nod and a smile and maybe some friendly conversation. Tricking is the most advanced social form we gay men have, a magic way to weave a web of intimacy through a diverse population. It's obviously more difficult to have a lover, but it can be done; there are some rules for how to do it. It's all the relationships and intimacies that fall in between that get so sticky. They are the ones that make you feel like a fool. There I was driving up I-95 with a hard on for a twenty-three-year-old I had met once and never been to bed with, and it didn't make any sense at all. But the hard on wasn't about to be denied. And I couldn't deny that I had let the boy/man slip past the line of "Trick" into the greyness whose only benefit is the experience of affection.

I stopped for gas and called him. It was freezing cold as I stood at the outdoor phone booth. "Can you call back, I'm in the shower." "No, I cannot call back, I'm in Rhode Island, for Christ's sake. Listen, will you be home this afternoon?" He hesitated. "I have class at five." "But are you free until then?" "Ummm…I guess so." Such enthusiasm! "Don't think you have to make any commitments now, I'll call you again when I get near Boston." "Okay."

Another hour and a half. I watched the dashboard clock tick away the minutes. There was another traffic jam in Providence where the freeway bisects downtown, and I grew increasingly impatient. I wanted to speed, but the road was littered with state troopers. I swore out loud at them.

I pulled into Boston and the neighborhood where I knew he lived. I called from another outdoor pay phone. Around and around we went. I was tired from the driving and he was hesitating about something. This was the same kid who called me only a week earlier to make sure we kept our connections up? Finally I said: "Okay. Something's going on and it doesn't work for us to fuck now. I know we only have an hour before you have to go to class. Maybe it insults you that I'd call for a quickie this way. That's all beside the point. I'm cold and tired and I want a cup of coffee. Can you make one for me, just to give us a chance to talk to one another?" Yes.

While I circled the block looking for a parking space it occurred to me that the idea of someone coming by and spending an hour over a cup of coffee might actually be more threatening than someone who wanted to come over and just fuck. He did have a lover, and the best way to keep a lover is to keep from having any competition in the special arena of intimacy. Tricks are for play, or so the philosophy goes. But for me, one of his most attractive attributes was that very lover. It was an insurance policy: a signal that this one was very unlikely to intrude on the intense privacy that is my controlled life.

By the time I parked the car and walked up the street to his address I had wiped all feelings of sex out of my conscious mind. I only wanted to explore who this boy/man was that he could attract me so strongly. I was going to have a cup of coffee and talk. He was standing on the street waiting for me as I approached his building. It was the first time I had seen him in daylight: he was beautiful.

He was standing on a concrete bench to be able to see the street from both directions. Hands in his pockets, his hair free from his cap, metal-framed glasses on his face. The same leather jacket over tight jeans. When he was sure it was me he smiled, flashing toothpaste-ad white teeth.

I felt another twinge of insecurity. I was bent over from the cold—my coat was back in the car. Not only was I unshaven and unshowered, I knew I was funky from driving straight through from New York. I was suddenly aware that I had only had coffee all day. The caffeine and more than a slight hangover were playing havoc with my usual calm. This was going to be difficult. I should have driven on to Portland rather than let him see me that way.

We walked up to his apartment, chattering about nothing in particular. He said he felt pretty bad about the phone calls. He thought he had been in the position of saying no all the time. (It was only twice, kid, give yourself a break.) We entered the apartment—it looked like two young gay men lived there with, I did see, perhaps a little better taste than most. I found a couple of books that indicated more substance than I expect from young clones.

I was glad I had already sat down when he took off his jacket. I had felt his body, but I hadn't seen it in the bar; I had no idea it was going to look like that. The tight t-shirt stretched itself over a prominent chest. It clung to his torso as it dove into a tight waist. The arms were heavily muscular with big bulges at the biceps. Wait a minute, I said silently, where did all this come from?

He went about making coffee, then came back and seemed to be making a new decision. He knelt on the floor in front of me and then leaned forward to kiss. I wasn't prepared. I had honestly made the transition and expected only that cup of coffee. His kiss was just as intense at home as it had been in the bar. He tasted sweet and his spit flowed freely, like juice; my crotch began to send its messages. "I thought we weren't going to do this," I muttered. He shrugged and smiled.

He pulled the shirt off over his head. His naked chest stunned me. There was a thick, unexpected patch of chest hair. The tits rose erect through the lush growth, little red nubs. The skin on his stomach was smooth and unblemished. Oh, arrogant youth! You have cause for your self-assuredness.

We embraced. Touching his body was like running my hands over fine silk and soft lamb's wool. The skin was tautly pulled over the hard muscles. Is there any touch as wonderful as that of young flesh? We kissed some more. He laid his head on my shoulder, turning his smile up to me. He was a beautiful boy/man; the hardness I had seen in the bar wasn't there right now. The cynicism and the snideness had been erased. He was looking at me with wide-eyed longing as he leaned his body on mine.

He stood and finished undressing. I thought back to *Rich and Famous* again and replayed the scene where the young hustler strips for Jacqueline Bisset. It was happening to me. Life imitates art. Art and life merge. *He was gorgeous.*

He knelt again. What were we going to do? Was the one-hour limitation so restricting that we could only have vanilla sex? Was his talk all air, or was he really looking for S&M? Then, a sharp, clear signal. He had an enormous cock, cleanly circumcised with big, meaty balls hanging beneath. Cock and balls were perfectly formed. But he wasn't touching them. His erection was full, and I could only begin to imagine how much he wanted to be playing with it. But he left it alone. He wouldn't move his hands there without permission. It is the type of thing that only a learned masochist would know about.

In the bars, leather is chic and S&M is hot. But most of the people only play at the games. They don't know the rules well enough to take themselves into the real inner circle. He was telling me: I know enough to be taken seriously. "You just might be as good at this as you claimed to be," I told him. He smiled with appreciation.

I reached and took his tits in my hands. The first night I had teased him about their being small and needing work. But there was certainly enough to grab hold of now. I pressed hard on each of them; a tiny gasp escaped from his throat. Too hard? His face went through a transformation. His eyes stared directly, defiantly into mine. Instead of pulling away he clasped my hands and goaded them on: further, harder. He thrust his chest forward: take them!

"You *are* very good," I said to reward him.

I released the nipples. He fell forward and nuzzled his face into my armpit. I flashed about my odor—there was so little time and I didn't want to break for a shower. But, no, he enjoyed the funk and rubbed his nose deeper. We kissed some more, and then stood to go to the bedroom.

I undressed while he sprawled out on the mattress. He had the body and face of a porno idol. There was no position he could put himself in that did anything but make him appear more handsome than before. His ass was a pair of beefy mounds, covered with more unexpected hair. I remembered telling him that I wanted to use a belt on his buttocks in the bar. Did we have time? Did I really want to? No and yes.

I shuddered at the first moment my entire body was placed against his. The size of that boy/man! The huge erection pressed between our bodies. I felt the strength of his arms and above all, always, wondered at the touch of that young skin. The muscles flowed easily from one to the next. There were curves in his sides and in his thighs that almost forced my hands to keep roaming over them.

The soft embrace lasted only a short time. My mouth went down his chest hair and found one of the beautiful little nipples. I began to chew. He took one of my hands and put it on the other tit as though he were making an offering. I nibbled at him with increasing pressure until I finally heard the little whimpers that announced my approach to the threshold of his actual pain. I lingered there for a short while, and then released him.

I placed him on his back and we began to kiss again. I climbed in between his legs and forced them apart with my knees. I could feel his balls, held tightly up against his pelvis by the retracting scrotum. My thrusting hips applied pressure on them. New sounds told me it was a special kind of pain. I lifted both of us roughly up onto our knees, then reached down and took hold of his balls. I squeezed, with gently increasing amounts of pressure, then broke off our kissing and stared at him. That defiant pride showed up on his face again. He sucked in his lower lip and bit. His hands submissively remained by his sides. He would be damned if he was going to give in.

I knew then just how far he would go to prove himself.

I could probably have done anything in the world to him if I wanted to; after that night in the bar he was going to be damned if he gave any evidence that he couldn't take it. He lunged his own hips forward, and I squeezed harder on his balls. He stared at me: do it, harder. I increased the pressure until his eyelids closed. Then I released him with a quick movement. A sharp intake of breath sounded; a sudden expression of fury looked back at me.

"Where's the grease?" He pointed to the can of Crisco on the table. I got it, then lifted up his legs. Now his face was full of anticipation. I probed my greasy cock in the hairy crevice between his cheeks and found his hole. My cock slipped inside. He moaned a little. I pushed further, until I could feel my cock sliding its length up his ass. The warm, sultry channel enveloped me. I was encased in his body. I was enraptured.

I rolled us onto our sides, my arms around my boy/man's chest. We kissed. His legs wrapped around my waist and I could feel their muscular bulk. He attempted to make it "hot." He started to move faster than I wanted to. I slowed him down. I pumped softly, gently, luxuriously in and out of his ass. His head collapsed against my shoulder again and he looked up at me. His mouth was barely open, his tongue played across the ridge of his teeth. I wanted him to call me "Daddy." I was desperate to hear the word, but it wasn't a scene I was used to playing out. Something was being touched inside me to create this strange fusion of sex and paternalism.

I changed the whole pace by pulling out of him without warning. Another flash of anger came over his face. "Roll over." There was so much defiance that I thought he might not do it. But then the heavy legs lifted themselves up and he turned. I grabbed his waist and lifted him till he was on his hands and knees, then guided my cock back into his ass. I pumped harder now. I reached around and took his cock in my grip. I could brush against the thick hair covering his balls while I slid my palm up and down his shaft. There seemed to be no part of his body that was less than perfect to my touch.

I coaxed his cock back to the erection it had lost. While I fucked and palmed him new words started to come out of him in soft whispers: "Yes, sir. Please, sir." I loved the sound.

I pulled out again, just as sharply as before. He turned on me with just as much anger. "Flat on your back." I felt like a lion tamer in a circus cage. The animal in him rebelled while it performed its commands. I moved over him and squatted down over his face; his tongue came up to meet my asshole. It lapped hungrily. The accumulated sweat of the hours-long drive must have been especially raunchy, but it didn't hinder him. He ate greedily. I reached down and grabbed his chest. I massaged his pectorals hard. I roughly tore at his tits. I looked at his cock: it was rigid in full erection. His hands were still obediently at his side.

I wasn't going to be able to hold out much longer. I laid my body down beside his and led his mouth onto my chest. He took in one of my tits, knowingly sucking it gently. I began to beat off while I whispered in his ear: "I'm going to come all over your face, boy. A big wave of cum all over you. I'm going to rub it in your hair and over your chin and make you lick it off my hand when I'm done."

His body was writhing with sex. I saw his hands. They were jerking in the air. I knew he was desperate to beat himself off. I could see all the need to start taking care of the pent-up pressure.

It was beautiful to see the control he was exerting as it came into conflict with his desire.

Random thoughts ran through my mind. Where did he learn this competency in S&M? What was going through his mind? What was his fantasy? Was he a slave boy in his dreams? Was he being raped by a stranger? Was I some glorified leather stud in his private melodrama? Or Daddy? Or a buddy? I wondered...I wondered.... I caught myself short. I wondered what was going to happen to him. If he was here, now, at twenty-three, what was going to happen later? I shocked myself with the sudden realization that I cared. I wanted to witness the boy/man come of age.

I pulled my nipple away from his mouth. "Please, sir, let me take your load." His mouth was wide open with his heavy breathing.

"I'm getting close, boy. When it shoots, you take this whole thing down your throat and swallow the last drop of it. I want it all the way down."

His hands were jerking again. I smiled at him. "Go ahead, boy, you can beat off." A fist raced to his shaft and began a melodic movement on his erection. His stomach muscles, sharply etched out, began to contract as his orgasm neared. Each of us kept coming closer and closer to the brink. I went over first. I reared up and thrust my cock down his throat just as I began to shudder waves of cum. His fist picked up speed and in only a few moments his whole body contracted and a puddle of white ooze splattered onto his belly, wetting the line of hair that ran down from his chest.

We fell back on the bed. His lips came up to mine and we kissed gently. His head rested on my shoulder. Again, I wanted to hear: "Daddy." But the little boy smile was sufficient for the moment. I ran a hand over his cheek, my fingers played with his moustache.

While I dressed he walked up to me with a magazine in his hand. He was shy. "Would you sign this?" It was an issue with one of my articles in it. I was pleased by his gesture. "Of course." I took pen and wondered what to write, then only signed my name. That was enough: it proved I had been there. Who I am and what I will be aren't decided, they don't need to be. I looked at his face and thought: "You are the most beautiful boy/man I have ever slept with."

I remembered reading a series of Japanese stories where the plots were all similar: People have such a perfect encounter with one another that when they part they vow never to see each other again. Perhaps that's what tricking should be. Perhaps it should be left unsullied by emotions. But, if I could get into that ass again…or, if he wanted me to witness his initiations…? He smiled, "I hope we have the chance to elaborate on this sometime later." So, youth takes the lead. I nodded, "We will."

I headed the car back onto I-95. For the rest of the journey back to Portland I thought about him. I wondered about all those random thoughts that cropped up during sex. There are so many needs and desires in life, and so few easy ways to have them fulfilled. There are so many ways to have sex and so few forms to allow that sex to develop into…relating. I couldn't find a better word.

The night fell as I drove north. The country became more and more familiar and more and more I felt I was coming home.

AUTHENTICITY

It happened in Provincetown last summer.

I was standing in a bar there, or what passed for a leather bar anyway. Not that I'm complaining about it—I've carried some great tricks out of there. But this was a slow night.

A couple guys had been following me around for the weekend. We'd always end up in the same places; they'd be at the beach when I was, poolside at the Boatslip, at Tea Dance.

They were as obvious as hell. The two of them must have made it their lives' work to collect the t-shirt of every leather bar in the country, and now it seemed like they were afraid to wear plain shirts for fear no one would see them if they didn't have a logo plastered across their chests.

So they changed maybe five times a day. They'd wear San Francisco bar shirts in the morning, Chicago bar shirts in the afternoon, New York bar shirts at Tea Dance, Washington bar shirts at dinner time, and Houston bar shirts at night. I felt like telling them, "I know, I *know* you're into leather bars."

They had begun to look like living Bob Damron guides.

They also wore an embarrassment of junk. They had every color handkerchief in the world. Keys, tit clamps, handcuffs, pieces of rawhide and an occasional dirty jock strap all hung from their belts at one time or another in those few days I had seen them.

Now, I don't mind that stuff; I wear some of it myself. But I have stopped being a promiscuous billboard about it. I mean, I wear enough to get my message across and the fact is the little things I wear do that quite nicely.

Even in a resort like Provincetown I still feel most natural wearing my engineer boots; my 501's are just part of my body by now; I've always worn a heavy leather belt and I think I might not know how to stand up straight if my keys weren't dangling on the left. If I'm going to carry a snot rag it might as well be black—and on the left.

Some other parts of me I can't help. I just appear a certain way to people. They tell me at home I look "severe." Not "handsome," not "attractive" but "severe." I guess part of it's the bushy eyebrows. Hereditary. So's the thinning hair. The close-cropped beard must goose the image along. So anyway, I'm not exactly *hiding* what I'm into. But, well, you can overstate this stuff.

I remember the good old bad days when being into leather was something special. I mean, it was something you had to get through to. It was the opposite of chic and if you admitted it was your scene you were telling the world something about yourself.

Now? Hell, if I want to assert my special sexuality when I go to New York these days I wear just jeans and a flannel shirt to a bar. Then they all think you must be really kinky.

That's what really got to me about these two guys: they approached it all so easily. I mean, I didn't have the slightest impressions that it meant anything to them to wear the shirts and the junkyard. It was only what was in for them.

When I was young it was a fearful thing to come on to a guy for rough sex. You were not really in danger, not if you had your street smarts about you and not if you knew anything at all about what was happening. But there was still mystery and excitement that was never there in regular sex. I couldn't sense any of that electricity in them.

It was inevitable that they would talk to me. They did, of course.

Even with all my ambiguity about their attitude I amazed myself. They were both hunky guys, they were hot, and they were after me, but I couldn't get that little flame burning in my crotch no matter what they said or I thought.

These two guys were offering me a guided trip around the world. I'm pretty heavy into sex. Wouldn't you think I'd get turned on? But I couldn't buy their ticket. I couldn't light the fire.

Part of it was the words they chose. They were all the right things, mind you, but I couldn't believe they were real words. They were statements these guys had read out of a magazine. That was it. They began with the usual bar talk, no problem there. But then they moved right into telling me about their scene in a very, very heavy way. And they did it without much caution.

I wanted to tell them to wait a minute, wait just a fucking minute! I had given them plenty of clues, I had talked about clubs I belonged to, places I'd been, things I'd read and the like.

They were treating it like cocktail chatter. It seemed to me that if you heard the credentials I had spun out you'd wait a few seconds before you started to talk about how much you'd like me to work over your tits.

The worst part? They bored me.

"I'd love to have you take me in a room and rip my clothes and made me suck your big fat cock," the first one said.

"Oh, yeah?" I took a swig of beer.

"I'd want you to make us call you sir and kiss your black leather boots," piped in the second.

"Really?" I leaned against the wall.

"You're the kind of guy that could turn us into real slaves. I just know you could."

"We'd have to do anything you wanted."

"We'd get our asses whipped if we displeased you."

I have to admit I yawned at this point. There was no passion in what they were saying. Their eyes sort of glazed over a little bit, but that was all. They were also talking more to one another than to me.

I felt like asking what was in it for me. I didn't bother—it was obvious I was just a prop in their fantasies. I can't get into that with bottoms. They're the kind who say, "A *real* master wouldn't do *that!*" Shit, what would these guys know about the real thing?

I let my eyes wander a bit. It didn't matter to the dynamic duo if I was looking at them or not; their tired litany kept on droning on and on, "…lick your ass…serve your body…drink your piss…."

Then I saw the kid on the other side of the bar. He was wearing ordinary clone clothes. Tight enough jeans, though they were a little too clean and new for my taste, but what the hell? A tank top, little running shoes, athletic socks. The shirt was close enough to his body that I could see his pecs. The tits weren't big enough to stand out from the rest of his chest. The arms bulged enough to be interesting. The ass looked gorgeous. He was staring at me with an intense, obvious interest.

I try to have good manners, but I just walked away from the other two to where he was standing. I think I must've left them in mid-sentence. I recall something about "...washing your armpits...."

"Hi."

He smiled back, the side of his mouth twitched a little bit.

Then the usual. Where are you from? Boston, he answered. And so it went. Till the clincher. He was the one who threw it out. "Where are you staying?" I gave him back the name of the guesthouse and added the expected, "Wanna come over for a while?" "Sure."

We started to walk through the crowd when an arm came out and grabbed him. I figured I was gonna have to listen to some kind of lover's quarrel, but the kid came right back out through the gang of people separating us and we walked out the door and onto the street.

We went up Commercial Street without saying anything until I finally asked him what that had all been about. "It was a friend of mine." The kid looked up at me. "He was worried." "About what?"

"That you might be more than I bargained for. He thought you might hurt me."

"What if I want to?"

He slipped an arm around my waist. "I don't know if I'd mind that much."

Now that little flame began to flicker. "Done much before?"

He shook his head. "Not really."

"What if I get carried away and start slapping you around?"

He rested his head on my shoulder as we continued towards the guesthouse. He barely whispered his reply. "No one's ever done it before." That was it. Not "No." Not "Please." Just an opening. The burning in my body was growing.

We walked into the house and up the stairs. I sprawled on top of the bed and lit a cigarette. He had given me the go ahead; I decided to take it. Nice and easy, with a steady voice, no dramatics, I said, "Take off your clothes so I can watch."

He was only a little stiff about it. I dragged on the cigarette and examined him as the shirt came off. His chest was rounded, his stomach firm. There weren't the muscles of a gymnast, just the natural tone of a nicely built guy in his early twenties. He kicked off the shoes and pulled off his socks. He undid his belt and hesitated. He looked up at me. Then he unzipped the jeans and pushed them down over his hips and calves till they fell on the floor.

His hard on was stuck in the folds of his jockey shorts. He looked at me again. A precious blush crept across his face as he stared at me. *Come on, kid, don't tighten up on me*, I encouraged him silently. This was a hard spot, one where they always had trouble. It's easy to have some stud rip your clothes off; it's hard to give in to a man and to expose yourself to the potential humiliation of this kind of self-exposure. I nearly cheered when he expanded the elastic band and stepped out of his underwear.

"Come here," I held out my arms and let him climb into them. There was that shock of the touch of flesh, young flesh. I kissed him, nice and soft, to reward him for a job well done.

I liked starting that way: him naked and me clothed. It underlines the roles, makes the position he put himself into more real. We made out for a while until I could feel his muscles relax. My hand went down and took his balls in my palm. They felt young, the eggy spheres seemed fresh. I didn't squeeze. I just wanted him to feel me hold him; I wanted the sensation of holding him for my own sake, too. He squirmed; it was a nice little wriggle, but he didn't try to move away. That was a good sign.

I leaned over and sucked in one of the little brown circles on the kid's chest. There was hardly any tip to it, just that nice satiny flesh. I rolled my tongue around and around. I could smell the young sweat from under his arms as its aroma wafted up at me. Then I started to bite. I just used little nibbles at first, the kind that anyone would enjoy; then I increased the pressure little by little.

I have to explain something about tits and me. I think men's nipples were put there to make life easy. There really is very little that works as well in S&M as tit play—unless you want to go all the way to some pretty heavy stuff. But those two little pieces of skin can evoke all the response and give all the sensations you need.

Pretty soon I had him moaning a bit. Not much, but enough honest little groans were escaping that I could tell he was really feeling it. I didn't slow down. In fact I increased the pressure some. "Please," he whispered eventually. I ignored him. I kept on teething his tit till the little nub was so tender that even my tongue could bring on the guttural sounds. Finally he tried to pull away.

I leaned up quickly and looked at him; I was resting my body on my left elbow. "What the fuck are you doing?"

He looked a tiny bit guilty and answered in a low tone, "You were starting to hurt."

"You knew what you were getting into. Want to leave?"

"No." He spoke that out loud.

I put a hand gently on his face. "Then put the other one in my mouth."

I laid back on the bed and watched him. There was the slightest hesitation. He looked down at his chest. It's always better to make them do things like this themselves, that way they can't get away with thinking you're forcing it on them. It's such a little thing, anyway, putting your nipple in a guy's mouth when you know he's going to work on it. But shit, I could see he had kept a hard on through everything that had gone on.

He gave in to that slight discipline and got up on his hands and knees and maneuvered his other nipple until it was right on the opening of my lips.

I repeated my little exercise on my new plaything, waiting for the moans. They came. I waited for the whispered "Please." It was spoken. I took him to that same place between pain and pleasure, but he didn't move away when he got there this time. Instead his hand came up and caressed my hair while I bit into him. When my mouth stopped working he thought I was done.

"Put the other one back here." I surprised him. He closed his eyes a little, just a little for a short while. Then he surrendered the already sore prize to my mouth.

Such a minor event, such a slight yielding—but I nearly came from the intensity of that moment between us. This time his hand immediately went to my head and he smoothed my hair while I continued this undistinguished torture. I kept it going from one nipple to the other until there was the sweet sound of a cry in his voice. I stopped and looked at his face just as a tear ran out of his eye. I licked it up. Then I kissed him.

That was when I undressed. I stood at the foot of the bed and let my hard cock jut into the air. "Come and take it." He got up and crawled to the waiting pole. I stopped his face just as he was about to swallow my erection. "Easy, just the head. Just put the head in your mouth till you get used to it."

He was very tanned, with a sharply defined line where his small bathing suit had protected him. He was on his hands and knees just barely holding my cock. The combination of his stance and his having my prick in his mouth was a picture of abject submission that turned me on more than I thought could be possible. It was really such vanilla. But so real, I thought, so real. It was the complement of my holding his balls; his letting my cock rest in his mouth.

I kept him that way until I thought he was probably getting bored. Not that I worried about that, actually: he was still rigid hard. The thing was, I wanted to take him to that place where he was unexcited, where he only thought about the hard cock in his mouth, not the excitement of exotic sex.

I didn't say anything to him. I just pushed him off my hard on and guided his body until he was on his back on top of the bed. I climbed up, spread over him and gave him another reward in the form of a long, deep kiss.

When I broke that off I looked into his eyes and told him the truth. "You're doing pretty good."

His eyes were wide open. His tongue wetted his lips. "I want to."

"I know, kid, I know."

There was only a quick kiss after that. I pulled back again. "You ready to go on?" There comes a point where you gotta make them say what you know they want to admit to. He nodded his head yes.

I crawled off him and sat at the edge of the bed, then manipulated his willing body until he was laid over my knees. "No one's ever hit you before, have they?"

"No."

I slapped him one very, very hard. Hard enough to get a yelp. "No what?"

He knew the answer right away. "No, sir."

I caressed the cheek of his ass that had a nice red mark from my hand. "That's my boy; you're learning."

You have to do it right. You have to build it up in them and on them. I started with nice little pats, hardly enough to make a sound. I let them alternate from one cheek of his ass to the next. But the constant repetition is what gets them, that and the almost undetectable increase in the severity and speed of the blows. They hardly have a chance to know that you've started to hit them if you do it well.

They get the final result of it all in any event. They get to the point where they start to move around. That's when there's a heat about it all. Their asses are burning from the spanking they're getting. Then they start to tense their buttocks. They try to defend themselves and try to convince themselves that their bodies can maintain their emotions. But your hand starts to hurt and you're really beginning to get to them if you go on.

Since you're starting to be a little less predictable as to when and where you're going to strike next they can't prepare themselves and they can't stop from letting out little boy cries of pain. They haven't a facade left; their whimperings are authentic emotions. It's a beautiful sound.

When I suddenly stopped he thought it was all over. I kept running my hand gently over the bright red surface of his ass. My palm tingled from the sharp contact that had gone on. I knew his buttocks felt at least as sensitive. It must have been a fine, cooling sensation for him to have that delicate touch after the long drawn-out spanking, but when he tried to act on his relief by sitting up I put a hand on his shoulder and said, "I'm not done."

His back stiffened with the shock of my words; I even wondered if maybe I wasn't going to lose him then. But there was this lovely little surrender that relaxed his whole body.

His tension returned when he realized that I was leaning over and grabbing at my pants to get that heavy belt of mine; he could hear it sliding out of the loops. I laid the cool leather on his ass and just let it rest there.

"You can tell me to stop now if you want to leave."
"No, sir."
"Does that mean you want me to belt you?"
"No, sir."
"Then what does it mean?"
"It means…it means you can do what you want to, sir."
Music, I tell you, music to my ears.

I doubled over the belt and started out slowly again. There was this beautiful man with his body wrapped around my lap and that back of his, those strong muscles just waiting to...but I stopped myself. I couldn't whip his back, not on the first time. He was only starting to realize the potential that his body held. I was helping him to look inside a part of himself that he had never glimpsed before. I wouldn't do any good if I unthinkingly burst open the barrier and frightened him. He was choosing now; nothing was being taken.

I kept at his ass with the belt. I never really let go, I just kept it up until the constant blows accumulated their force. I felt his arms as they tightened around my knees and his face as it started to press against my thighs, first just rubbing, then moaning, then the squirming, then the yells he couldn't have restrained and then, finally, the sounds of the sobs as he broke.

I put the belt away and reached down to kiss the glowing skin, I rubbed my face against the heat of his flesh and knew that there would be marks the next day. Not deep welts some people aspire to, but the black and blue memories of the physical encounter.

I gathered him up and once more spread him on the bed. I kissed him again. A bit of pride in him came over me. "You're doing pretty good for a guy who's never been around."

There were still little pools of tears around his eyes. Yet his smile came through all the same. "Thanks...sir."

Then I fucked him. I fucked him long and hard and pleasantly. It took all my self-discipline to keep from shooting real early in the game, but I held back until I knew, I *knew,* he understood that that cock of mine was plowing him. Only then did I let go and let an earthquake of cum pulse out of me and into his belly, leaving my seed deep in his gut.

When I was done and had pulled out I rolled onto my back. "Climb up here," I patted my belly. He was a little puzzled. I put my arms behind my head. "Beat off while I watch you."

It was a beautiful sight. He straddled my midsection and worked his cock into a full erection. He was looking down at me and pumping away at his cock. His hips would involuntarily rise and fall with his growing turn-on. I loved the sight—especially when I saw him put one hand behind himself and I knew he was feeling the heat on his ass.

"Come on, kid, come on," I whispered to him, coaxing him on. It's hard for guys to masturbate in front of someone sometimes. But it's just like everything else, they have to learn how to do it. "Want some more leather on your ass?" I teased.

"No," he hissed but I noticed that the speed of his pumping hand increased.

"Are you sure you don't?"

He opened his mouth, but instead of an answer in words I only heard a gasp of his clenching orgasm. His stomach muscles tensed and then there was a torrent of hot cum splashing onto my chest with throbbing waves.

His body half collapsed with relief; his head hung down with exhaustion. I ran my hand through the cooling ooze and took it up to his mouth. He didn't open his eyes, but his lips parted and his tongue came out and licked at the masculine liquid.

I wouldn't have stopped there with someone more experienced. But I let the kid relax then. Hell, he'd been through more that night than any other since he'd come out, or so I figured. I let him cuddle up to me and we felt the cum dry between us.

We showered. The sight of that pretty ass when he bent over was enough to nearly make me want to start all over again. Later, I thought. Maybe another day. I just luxuriated in the idea of how much he had given me and of how I had been a unique moment in his life.

I thought the whole trip had taken maybe an hour. But while we were dressing I looked at the clock and realized we had just gone through four hours of non-stop sex. He was late to meet friends at the disco downtown, and we joked about what they probably thought I had done to him.

I walked him down Commercial Street and pointed out a shortcut to the dancing bar he wanted to go to. A little peck from him and a wave and off he went. I fingered the piece of paper with his name and address and looked forward to a trip to Boston.

It was too late to do much of anything but go on to the bar.

The pair was still there. Or, I should say, they were there again: they must have gone home since they had changed their t-shirts. Philadelphia leather bars were getting the free publicity tonight.

They came up to me as though I were a magnet. I tried to keep the conversation nice and low-key: Where had they eaten dinner? Had they tried this other place yet?

One of them went off to the john. The other took quick advantage of the situation. "Look, my lover's not nearly as heavy as I am. If that's what turned you off, I'll get rid of him for the night."

"No, no, I'm fine."

"Please, Master, please." There still wasn't anything in that voice, damn it. Nothing. But there was no stopping it either. "I'll gladly serve your body with my tongue. I'll lick your ass. I'll be your human toilet paper...." There was no edge to it; he was just telling me things he'd be willing to do with anyone. There might, someplace, be something that he hadn't experienced before, but I knew he'd never show it to me. He had a good body and I guess I would have been willing to play with it some other time in my life, but if I did he wouldn't even be conscious of who I was while I did it. He'd be having fantasies that had nothing to do with me.

The other one came back. He didn't get mad at me but he was honestly confused about something. "Why'd you trick with that vanilla kid? He wasn't such hot shit. We could've given you a much better time of it than he could. Man, I'd really like to be able to drink your piss...."

"...while I licked your asshole...."

"Ah, shit," I said under my breath and walked away from them.

It had started to rain in the few minutes I'd been in the bar. But, I figured, the fuck with it. I walked up to the dancing bar and paid a ridiculous cover charge to get in. I don't think I'd even been there that whole summer till that night.

I walked to the edge of the dance floor and saw him out in the middle of it, paired with an attractive clone number. It only took a few seconds before he spotted me standing there waiting for him. He said something to the other guy and left him dancing by himself. When he got to me he put his arms around me. "My tits hurt," he laughed.

"Complaints?"

"No way." He kissed me, then put his head against my chest and his arms tightened around me.

"I want to go home and go to bed. Come with me." It wasn't really an order, but…well, let's just say I was pretty definite. "Go tell your friends we're leaving."

As we climbed the stairs to the guesthouse I asked him, "What'd you say to the guys you were with?"

He smirked. "That my lover showed up unexpectedly and I had to go with him."

What the hell? A fantasy's a fantasy.

That night he slept in his jockey shorts with my arms around him.

METAMORPHOSIS

Just because you get older, it doesn't mean you get smarter, nor that you necessarily see everything that's going on around you. It's especially hard to remember to watch for the little things, the subtle alterations—anyone can catch the obvious. When a disco doll puts on a leather jacket there's no ignoring it. When a truck driver gets into drag it doesn't go unnoticed.

I go down to Provincetown every year for at least a few weekends off season. I've been doing it for twenty years, since I was seventeen. As different a place as P-town is it still has many of the characteristics of a New England village. I, being a born-and-bred Yankee, react to it just the same way my parents still react to their hometown in Massachusetts.

One thing that means is that newcomers of any kind are ignored for a while. Like when I moved to Maine: I knew I'd have to be there for a couple winters before the locals would take me seriously. Sure, you can be hot and get picked up and laid but if you're going to be a part of the community you have to…well, pay your dues.

They come and go in Provincetown like colors in a sunset. My friends who live there and I will sit on the front stoop of their house and watch them parade up and down Commercial Street every year. We'll listen to them make big plans to spend the rest of their lives on the Cape. Sure, we nod, we know. Most of them don't last more than two summers—or I should say, one winter.

Provincetown may be a carnival from Memorial Day to Labor Day, but it's a quiet little town the rest of the year. The guys who do stay there have to be able to find beauty in the barren beaches during the fall and the shifting sands during the winter when the dunes move across the highways and block traffic as though they were snowdrifts.

I think you'd have to be pretty happy with yourself if you were committed to living in Provincetown year round. Probably you'd need a lover to make it through the cold season. The people who live there usually have to lunge for the sun sometime during those long months; many of them go down to Florida or west to California for at least part of their off-season. They read a lot; watch too much television; spend a lot of time alone.

I'm one of a certain kind of person that exists in New England towns, especially resort communities. I don't limit myself to summer trips to the Cape; I'm something of a regular, but not enough of one to ever have been a resident. It makes for a nice situation, like I have another community than my own. My face shows up often enough that people recognize it and say hello to it even if they haven't ever met me. I get to go to the parties, pick the hot tricks, pick up a free beer from the bartenders, all the little things. And, of course, the people in town are as familiar to me as I am to them.

So I go down and spend my time with my friends and I know where the cheap liquor is kept and that I'm not supposed to use the fancy bottle that's really just for show. I long ago stopped asking about eating out of the refrigerator and just make a sandwich out of whatever I choose. I see the milk's getting low and I go out and buy a gallon for the house.

I watch the kids come and go and I get to know the guys that stay. We eat pastries at the Portuguese bakery and have dinner at the Lobster Pot; we stand around Tea Dance when it's on and go over to the bars later in the night.

There is a bit of me that keeps some of them away. My friends just learned to accept it long ago. You know how it is with long-term friends: they just take all the parts of you in with the complete package and stop worrying about those things that aren't quite what they might like. My little thing is heavy sex. My friends have this very nice guesthouse, loaded with antiques. I think in the beginning they were worried that the sounds of leather on flesh would mean broken vases or marred woodwork. They got over it. They'd just watch the guys I'd take up the stairs and smile. Actually, they got used to asking a lot of questions later on, the next day—especially if the number was hot.

But New England accepts peculiarities and makes few judgments in private. If you needed to act out your fantasies on the sidewalks then the Yankees would scream and yell and the Portuguese would have fits at the next town meeting. But I suspect that my walking up and down Commercial Street made no waves after a while.

About five years ago I met a new kid in town. He was surprisingly tall and surprisingly handsome. Bill. He had come to live with the owner of another guesthouse, someone I'd known for a few years. I wasn't sure what their thing was together—still I don't know—but I just took to Bill for some reason. Nice kid. Sometimes my friends would get caustic about him, not that they didn't like him, they just wanted him to pay his dues I guess. But I'd come to his defense. That surprised them; I usually didn't do that.

One day, the first summer we were both in town, I was taking some photographs. I knew I could sell some to a skin mag if I could get a couple models, and I thought of Bill. I went over to his house and asked if he and a friend of his wouldn't mind posing in bathing suits for me. He seemed stunned. I thought he was going to get all upset about people seeing him in a gay photograph, but no, he agreed.

I just needed a couple bodies on the sand. No big thing. I posed the two of them in different positions making them appear to be boyfriends or something like that. They had fun doing it; I got my pictures.

I bought them a couple beers afterward to thank them and we talked a little bit. Bill commented that he felt funny about modeling. There was that discomfort I had felt earlier again. Why, I asked him—you're handsome, a big guy, hot, why shouldn't someone take your picture?

It was time for true confessions after I opened up the subject that way. Seems Bill used to be a lot bigger. Well, he's the one who used the word "fat" so I suppose I can too. He'd just shed something over a hundred pounds before he moved to Provincetown that spring and was still dieting.

It was a little awkward for me. I had seen his body in the bathing suit and I had seen the lack of tone in his flesh. There were parts of him that just hung. The sudden loss of weight made sense as the cause of it all. It seemed a shame a man with his handsome face wouldn't have a better body.

The summer went on after that. Bill got a job tending bar at the biggest gay place in town and his friendly manner made him popular. I'd stand in the corner and watch him. I never thought much more than, "Nice kid."

Bill's lover was into some kink, I never really explored what kind. Over the next few years though I saw some changes in Bill, mainly in his clothing. Little things I'd notice just every once in a while. The appearance of a red handkerchief in his right-hand pocket. A key chain…on the right. A leather vest. But the accumulation of things was gradual; it didn't stand out in my mind.

I'd come and go to Provincetown. You could never say what part of the season I'd be there. But Bill was always working that bar; it was the only gay place that stayed open all year round. I'd be there in my corner, usually wearing my leather chaps and such and hunting for my special kind of prey. Every time I walked in Bill'd give me a beer and we'd say hello, exchange some quick gossip if it wasn't too busy.

There must have been some longer conversations in there. I remember once I went to P-town with a trick and we stayed in Bill's lover's house. The trick wanted to get fisted; I don't really like to do it and I left the three of them there for some ass play one night. Maybe we talked about it.

My friends would make some comments about Bill every once in a while. At first they were simply appreciative thoughts like my own. Later on they had an edge to them that I could see only with hindsight now. "What'd you think of Bill this visit?" "Nice kid," I'd say.

Then this last summer I went down for July 4th. When I had lived in New York it seemed foolish to go to P-town on a holiday weekend in the summer. But living in Maine puts a different complexion on everything. I had felt like I'd be trading one circus for another if I flew to Cape Cod from Manhattan. Now I go there just for that very show.

One Saturday night I put on my leather and went to say good-bye to my friends. I told them I was going to the big party at the Boatslip, then maybe to another bar. "Have fun," one said. The other looked at me with a little sneer, "Seen Bill this trip?" "No," I replied. "You will."

Now *that*, I thought, was strange.

A friend from Boston met me and we went over to the poolside party. It was one of the big costume events they have every year. They're okay things; sort of Provincetown goes Fire Island for the night. Okay, but not a big deal. I was in chaps and jacket, handcuffs hanging from my waist, heavy leather boots. He was in a cop outfit. The queens around us thought we had the perfect getups for the party; we didn't have the heart to tell them it was what we would have worn any night.

There's only so much of what we could take of that kind of party. It was a benefit and we really were just there to give the kids some support and a couple bucks; once we'd done our duty we made our way over to the leather bar.

We were standing there having a beer and checking out the possibilities when Bill walked in. It was a shock. I realized I had never seen him in a bar except the one he worked at and there

I'd seen him only on duty. He walked up to me and said hi.

"What're you doing here?" I didn't mean to interrogate him, but it seemed worth asking.

"The party's cut business into shreds everywhere but here. Who wants to dance at a disco when all the others are at the benefit? So I talked the manager into giving me the night off."

"Good enough," I said.

I stood there and looked at the groups and tried to pay attention to my friend and Bill as they had some kind of conversation. I was horny that night. Not just horny for sex; I was hot. I wanted someone who knew what was up, someone I didn't have to play games with but could get down to some serious business with. There were a couple possibilities, but they didn't look promising.

I felt a strange hand on my hip just then, gliding over the leather of my chaps. I looked up to see who it could be; there wasn't anyone around me. Then I realized it was Bill. His hand was simply caressing the animal skin on my leg, softly, invitingly.

I was momentarily uncomfortable. This kid had been a little part of my life for the last five years. I had never come on to him, he hadn't come on to me. Now the hand.

I stood still and just let it happen. We were right at the bar and a couple more rounds of beer came our way before anything was said. I wasn't feeling too much pain by now. What I was feeling, though, was a hard on trapped in my jeans. That palm was working wonders.

The other friend left, and now I had to deal with Bill. We were alone and he had turned to face me eye to eye. He smiled a little and came even closer. He kissed me. Just a peck, no tongues. His hand moved and cupped my crotch; he must have felt my erection. He removed the hand and pressed his own body against mine. The hard on he had was just as obvious to me as my own was.

I was waiting, waiting to hear what he was going to say. A quick fuck in my room? A blow job on the dunes? I was surprised the kid was turned on to me; I remembered that body from a few years ago and couldn't get turned on by my image of it. But I liked the kid. I liked the hand on my crotch. I liked his face close to mine and the taste of his lips, and if he wanted sex, we'd do it.

"I know you're not into fisting, *sir*," he emphasized the last word. "But—just for tonight—why don't you believe the handkerchief in my pocket's black, not red. Black as the night."

My spine stiffened as erect as my cock. I felt my face harden. "Don't play that game with me unless you mean it."

His smile went. Seriousness took its place. "I mean it. And I know what it means." His hand left my crotch and he fingered the handcuffs that fell from my belt loops. "I sure do...*sir*."

I grabbed him by the hair on the back of his head and yanked him toward me. Our mouths were open now; the kiss was sloppy and the tongues were anxious. I jerked him away from me. His mouth opened in pain from the sudden pull on his hair. "Let's go."

We walked the short distance to his place. He had his own room in the guesthouse for playing, he told me. We got there and I sprawled on the mattress. I was tired; it was late; there had been a lot of beer that night.

He stood at the foot of the bed and played with the top button of his shirt. He was smiling again. "I suppose I should tell you something." He undid the top button. "This winter," the next button, "I started," the shirt front was now undone, "to work out." Like a trained stripper he pulled open the shirt, then ran a hand up and down his stomach.

It was beautiful. Darkly tanned from the early summer days on the beach, the skin was pulled tautly over an expanse of muscle. Horizontal ridges of hardness covered his belly. A burst of bulk proclaimed his pectorals. His arms were sculpted. He knew it. He knew he had turned himself into something wonderful.

The pants came off next. His thighs were tough with sinew; his calves defined with ropy muscles. He turned enough for me to see the ripples of his back and the hard roundness of his ass.

This was not the boy I had met years ago; this was someone new. He climbed onto the bed smiling the whole time. My arms went around him and felt the smoothness of his tight flesh.

Now, with a cute little change, I was the one who was entrapped. While we were walking home I had been conjuring up images of a scene I could go through with him. Not any more. I could only feel the masculine body and be surprised that it had fallen into my grasp.

We kissed. Just a little. He looked up. "Anything you want, sir, anything at all." But as bottoms usually do, he was telegraphing his desires clearly. His hand was holding the handcuffs, his eyes were lingering on the belt around my waist.

I stood up and stripped naked, then I spread my body over his. The touch of male beauty was so powerfully erotic I forgot the beers and the fatigue. Our cocks were hard and rolled against one another. I pressed a thigh into his balls and felt their fleshy mass,

We were wrapped tightly against one another; every possible inch of each of our bodies fought for contact with the other. He wasn't grappling for control; that was perfectly plain, especially once his arms raised up above his head and presented his chest in a pose of utter subjugation. But he had a favor to ask. "Sir, would you put your leather back on?"

I stood again and grabbed the chaps, pulling the cool leather over my naked legs. I found the vest and dragged it over my back, then I slipped into my boots, "This is what you want?"

"Yes, *sir!*"

I went back through my pile of clothes and found my pants. I took the handcuffs off their loop and pulled out the belt. I doubled it over and laid it across his chest. "Still sure?"

"Yes, sir."

He was compliant as I manipulated his body onto his stomach. I attached his wrists with the metal, then dragged him onto the floor on his knees. My cock waved in front of his head and he went for it. I smacked him across the face. "When I tell you to."

I put him chest down on the mattress, letting him support himself on his knees. The belt did its work. Sometimes men moan with delight when you go at them. Sometimes they yelp in real—or mock—pain. But seldom do men accept a whipping as enthusiastically as Bill did.

He wasn't content to tell me his feelings. He acted them out. His ass would rise up to greet each blow. His legs would twitch with appreciation whenever the belt struck them. He never moved away from it but seemed to actually try to anticipate where each of the strokes would hit him.

When I finally stopped I didn't have a chance to see the fine lines of red on his flesh. He swiveled around quickly and pressed his face against the leather of my chaps. He tongued them greedily.

I reached over and picked up the candle he had lit when we had entered the room. I grabbed his hair with my free fist and pulled him backwards against the mattress. His eyes focused on the candle, the white wax melting. He just said, "Yes."

He watched with intense interest as the candle moved more closely to his body. It was directly over his chest when I finally tipped it and let a slight stream of melted wax dribble onto his chest. The stream hit almost directly onto his right nipple, sending waves of sensation across his body.

I pulled the candle back and watched his face: he was staring at his tit with an expression of wonder. "Man, beautiful, beautiful, sir." It was barely a whisper.

I brought the candle back and repeated the ministration on his left nipple. His mouth was open. On any other man I would have said it was pain, but the brightness of his eyes reflected awe. I'll never know if it was directed towards me, or if it was his own astonishment with himself, but he never tried to draw back.

I fucked him later, after having chewed the heat-sensitized nipples and having caressed the big testicles with a powerful grip that came the closest of anything to taking him too far. The fucking was good. We slept soundly, though we didn't close our eyes till long after the first sign of dawn.

He wasn't in the bed when I woke. I stretched and listened to the chatter of the guests as they walked up and down the hallway on their way to breakfast, the beach, whatever. There was a hint of a hangover in my tiredness. I wanted a shower to wake me up, but thought better of it. He must have gone on to do his errands, I supposed; there had been nothing in the night together that could have caused him to leave unhappy.

I lit a cigarette and stayed there for a while. Just as I was dragging on the butt he opened the door and came in carrying a hot cup of coffee, with a big grin on his face. "Morning, sir."

I took the coffee, smiling at his overstated use of the title. He sat on the side of the bed, giving me an opportunity to caress him some more. "I've never seen this body before."

"I told you I'd been working out."

"Not till you got me home."

He shrugged, pleased with his game. "I've wanted to do that for years. *Years.* I'd watch you across the bar and look at the leather and the tricks you'd drag out of the place. I'd always want to be the other guy.

"You know, it's not just 'cause of the leather. That turned me on, no question. But there was something else." He stretched and I could see new, hard muscles in the bright daylight. He was feline—no, more than that, it was the grace and strength of a leopard that I saw in his torso.

"Remember when you took those pictures a few years ago?"

"Of course I do."

He was quickly but deeply pensive. "You don't know what it's like to grow up fat and ugly. It was like a defense, though. It made sure I didn't have to face being sexual. Hell, who'd want a tub like I was? When I gave up the flab, I gave up the defense. That's when I moved to Provincetown.

"It was good. I met my lover and moved in. I made a life for myself. I don't do too badly. But it wasn't until you took the pictures that I even thought I was attractive—or that I could be.

"Posing for those few photographs was the biggest ego boost

I ever got. I just had never thought of someone looking at me that way. And when they came out in the magazine, I couldn't believe it. I was so used to avoiding my reflection in the mirror I guess I just couldn't stand the idea of looking at me. But there I was, and there were all these people around the country who saw me.

"Do you know I got phone calls?" I shook my head. "You mentioned the guesthouse and people'd call and ask to talk to me. *Me!*

"So…I took over. I figured I had more than I realized. It wasn't just this past winter; I'd started before. But with the cold season there's not much else to do, so I got a really pro set of weights and put them up in the house and I'd sweat and strain and struggle with them every day.

"When you came back this summer I knew I had to show you what I'd accomplished." He spread his arms, the pectorals bulged out, the triceps defined themselves. "And I figured somehow you had a place in the start of it. You might as well get in on the end."

We laughed and kissed and I hugged him. "Besides," his voice had gone to a whisper, "I've always wanted to know what it'd be like to wear those handcuffs and lick that leather."

I still see Bill every time I go to Provincetown. I'll stand in the corner and watch him tend bar. His t-shirts have gotten tighter; more reason to show himself off. He's still friendly as can be and he still gives me a beer now and then.

Whenever I see him with someone I wave and think to myself that the other guy really should find a chance to thank me for my own part in what's happened. It's a good feeling.

INTERLUDES

Michael and I were standing in the Mineshaft. It was a quiet night. Snow was falling heavily and only those that Michael called "The Committed" had bothered to make the trip to this sex-palace, hidden deeply inside the meat-packing district that's a no-man's-land between the Village and Chelsea.

When he walked in we didn't even pay attention to him. We didn't even acknowledge that we had noticed him; there was no need to. It went without saying that everyone would admire him.

He had crossed the room to the coat check. There he not only left his black leather jacket, but he also took off his shirt and left his upper torso bare except for the stark leather harness that crisscrossed his chest and back. He got a beer at the bar and stood not far from us.

It's perfectly understandable to me that I thought he was unavailable. The body that stood in front of us was obviously the result of enormous effort: the muscles that rippled over his back and the biceps that bulged on his arms were no natural development, but were the result of years of work. After all that labor I just assumed that he would want to have an encounter with an equally devoted bodybuilder.

Michael wandered and I stayed in the bar sipping my own beer. The man didn't move. I studied him with cool detachment; I thought of him as a model. It was an easy and safe manner for me to judge him since I'm a sometime photographer. From that perspective he was possibly even more handsome than he had been as a gay male standing in a sex bar. I could sense the proportions he had built himself to, the extent to which he had carefully stayed just this side of the grotesque with his bulk.

What was impressive—beyond his artificially constructed musculature—was the texture of his skin. I could see it in the flattering red light he stood under. It was unblemished, unflawed, stretched tightly over his body as though he had just that night worked out to pump the brawn for public viewing.

He wore a black handkerchief in his right pocket. I smiled and thought that the whole bunch of men there must have sighed with disappointment when they had seen that. It's seldom that a magazine image comes to life so totally in a gay bar. This was a man with whom they probably would have adored living out some fantasy.

The night was only beginning and I was only vaguely horny. I had decided to wait a few more minutes before I walked around; perhaps I'd have another beer. It was just about then that he turned and came up to talk to me.

I went through the well-rehearsed replies to his banter. He lived in New York; I was from Maine. We talked about occupations and social activities. We wondered if we knew mutual friends. All through this exchange I didn't realize that he was coming on to me.

I can't recall the exact moment when I understood. It was a shock; I do know that. I smiled at my reactions. Here I was, supposedly some kind of seasoned pro in the world of gay sex, and I didn't even know the prize was mine for the asking.

My attitude changed only a bit. I tested his interest and he confirmed that I wasn't fooling myself. Soon he slipped easily into calling me "sir." Each of the first times he used the title he would look me directly in the eye as though he needed to communicate a special intent with the word.

My hands explored his body. The muscles felt even better than they had looked. Each probe on my part was matched by some movement by him. We kissed. It was long, wet, lingering. I took the beer from his hands after we had set the roles clearly. "My boots," I said. He dropped immediately to his knees, his arms went behind his back and his head onto the scruffed black leather. I could feel the pressure of his tongue against the worn surfaces.

It was meant to be a sudden and quick order of some severity. It was an examination—I had to gauge how much he meant all the small signals of submission that he had conveyed with words. His actions gave them meaning. He knelt willingly and obediently in front of an audience of anxious onlookers and calmly and compliantly accepted my wish.

I brought him back to his feet; I had no need to humiliate him further. Not now. I kissed him again. Grains of dirt from my boots were on his lips. When I broke the embrace he softly laid his head against my chest. "Thank you, sir."

I interrogated his body further. I couldn't find a single point of resistance; there was no pain I could inflict that he would refuse willingly. There was no affection I could offer that he did not accept greedily.

We went to a corner of the bar. I pulled at him, punched at him, fingered him, gnawed him. He stayed with me: I would kiss him and pry open his mouth. His tongue rushed to greet mine. Then I took him to a table in the middle of the room and spread his body out in front of the crowd. I took my belt and beat his ass, his thighs, his back. He did not rebel.

I dragged him into the back room of the Mineshaft and ordered him to grab hold of a crossbeam. There he waited. A crowd gathered and appreciated his beauty. I ran my hand up his side and into his armpit where I gathered the sweat of the strain, the fear, the excitement. He waited, knowing I would beat him more.

There was no part of him that was less than magnificent. His buttocks were as hard as his biceps; his chest was etched with fine lines of muscle. The men who crowded us couldn't help but try to touch him. Even while my belt thudded on his back their hands would reach out and worshipfully attempt to feel some part of him.

They were awesomely silent. It was as though a new, precious icon had appeared in this house where men were venerated.

While I could understand their reverence and the respect their touch represented, it broke the finely tuned communication between us. He was not there—I could tell this—to gather their admiration. He had come to offer himself up to a single man and he had chosen me. These others violated his act of submission.

"Let's go back to the front," I whispered in his ear as I pulled his arms down. I could feel the heat my belt had left on his ass and back and I could hear the troubled breathing that proved how much the leather had inflicted on him.

"Yes," he kissed me just a little.

People followed us from room to room hoping that the ritual this man and I were performing would be repeated. They stood and stared while we got beer and went back to our corner.

There are always attractive men at the Mineshaft; there are always gay men who have strained for years to create a body. But there was no one quite so near perfect as he that evening. The onlookers thoughtlessly groped themselves as they spied on us.

We had left them behind. We had moved into a new passion. It isn't enough to say we kissed more; we did much more than that. We talked, our bodies intertwined and our mouths touching each other's constantly. My hands roamed wherever they pleased. If they ever indicated the slightest desire to explore someplace where it was difficult to maneuver, he would move to accommodate them.

He told me a great deal about himself. His work, his schooling, his sexuality all were described. He had—this was obvious—had a great deal of experience in S&M. He had had a master once, years ago in another city. Now he was living with another man but their sex life was going, nearly ended. He was obviously very sad and very lonely about it.

There are times when a man has such an obvious attribute that it must be commented upon. To not notice is to be as ridiculous as it would be to pretend to ignore an infirmity in other people. I had to ask him about his physique. I am not uncomfortable with my body; I am hardly insecure in a gay bar where everyone's appearance is judged. But I wanted to know why he would give me this when I was clearly not a match.

He looked away for a little while. "I told you I had a master once. When it was over, when he couldn't see me any more, I realized how much I had felt inadequate. I decided that I should at least have a body to give a man who might come along in my life and claim me. There might be," he looked at me with that deep intent he had used when we first talked, "another master and when he comes I want him to have something from me that he would not only desire, but take pride in."

He stepped back. He presented himself for visual inspection. He cocked his head, his clean-shaven face looked soft in the reddish light, the short hair gleamed, the skin of his chest was banded with the leather from his harness. "Do you like it, sir? Does it please you?"

"I like it very much." I drew him into my arms.

Just as we had challenged and matched one another physically, so did we now emotionally. I probed his mind and found a great loneliness. His lover's withdrawal was reminding him of too many other rejections.

We talked for hours. Occasionally the lust that flowed between us would take over and he would kneel to suck my cock or bend to feel my hand on his ass. Each time he would race back to my arms to thank me, to be comforted, to continue.

Once you get into someone's mind that way you learn the fine distinctions each individual has for what others might think of as universals. To that man his body meant something very particular, as did his leather and his willingness to be kissed.

Any two men can take any action and define it for themselves. Many men—perhaps hundreds—watched the two of us that night. Many men thought they saw a master and a slave. They wouldn't see the layers of interaction.

When I had explored his needs and fantasies I had the choice of leaving them alone or of picking them up and embracing them. I could have insisted that we return to the level of anonymous sex partners; I'm sure he would have gone along with that demand. I could have turned away when I discovered his loneliness. I didn't have to accept that discovery; I hadn't offered to find that by being in a sex palace. But that wasn't the way it worked.

We slipped out of our leather fantasy and entered a new one that had such intensity for him, it couldn't be taken for a game. He dropped "sir"; he began to call me "Daddy." He would slide in and out of the dream world, one moment talking about his day-to-day life and the next laying his head against my body to ask for acceptance, even healing.

It was inside me to find the strength to match his need. He was joyous. His lustful kisses became little pecks of gratitude.

His talk and his actions lured me into his world. Men have given me their bodies before and I have certainly taken pride in them. I have constructed whole dreams with some men. But I couldn't quite remember anything as complete and credible as this man's. I became, in my mind that night, his father. I draped a proud arm around his shoulders. When I finally fucked him I did it with an incestuous passion.

It was very, very late. Michael was standing nearby, obviously waiting to drive me back to our hotel. I had to leave. The boy and I exchanged names and addresses; he promised to visit me soon. At the last moment I tore up the slip of paper he had given me. "No, it's up to you to contact me."

He didn't write for months.

I was surprised. More than that I was disappointed. The source of my disappointment was myself, not him. When sex takes place in the realm of intense fantasy then either partner has the right to leave it there and not return. It may well be the sign of great wisdom to do so. But the exciting times are those when the fantasy and the reality merge to some extent and when they are able to inform one another—when the sex isn't isolated it can affect the rest of the experience.

I tried to explain this to Michael, but he didn't understand the extent to which it mattered to me. He had only seen me beating a man in the Mineshaft.

Finally the man wrote. It was a tenderly tentative letter. The months that had passed had included a point of no return with the lover who had left him; there would be no reconciliation. In his loneliness he wanted to visit me. "If it's too much to ask, I understand." But he also reproduced sensations from that night. "I have not forgotten your face or cock or the force with which you drove my mind into a dripping cave." And the emotions, "I need a Daddy who can caress his boy and tell him everything will be all right."

There were letters and phone calls. Arrangements had to be made and time had to be secured. When it was finally settled and I stood at the airport and waited for the arrival of his flight I was in a state of great anticipation.

I watched him walk off his plane and onto the pathway to the terminal. He couldn't have seen me in my perch on the walkway above him. I followed as he walked into the lobby and stood looking around the reception area. I went up to him and could see the look of question on his face. It had been months; he was unsure of himself. I could imagine his doubts about being there. It must have been difficult, I thought, for a young man to admit such great need that he would turn to someone he had met once, fucked with once, and that only in a sex bar. Great need, or great belief in that night.

We carried his bags to the borrowed car and I took him to my apartment. In my dreams I had used his body in violent ways, taking it always to the sexual extremes I had forced at the Mineshaft. But the uncertainty he exhibited was too gentle to be assaulted. We talked easily as I drove, and when we arrived we sat at the table and drank a beer as he told me about the last few months of his life.

Much of his identity had been tied up with the lover who had gone. He felt anchorless and, more, he felt unappreciated. Conversation wasn't going to be enough to reassure him.

He wanted to shower. Of course, I said, and I took him to the bathroom. The stall had opaque glass doors. I took a seat in the next room from which I could look directly at the shower. He stripped, glancing at me occasionally. We chatted. I smoked a cigarette while he climbed in and turned on the water. The slight, nebulous vision of his body was erotic. The glass soon was steamy from the hot water and the outlines of his physique were blurred. The bulk of his muscles was still evident, the curve and the mass of his buttocks were all the more sensual by their ability to be seen in such an unclear view.

He turned off the water and climbed from the stall, and toweled himself while he talked more to me. When he was dried he started to walk through the room toward the front of the apartment where he had left his clean clothes. But I grabbed him and took away even his terrycloth covering. I brought him to me and sat him on my lap. His chest was directly in front of my face. I sucked in one of the nipples and rolled it with my tongue.

A hand came to my neck and pulled me hard against him. He kissed my forehead. When I stopped he touched his lips to mine. "I haven't had sex in a long time, because of my lover, " he said shyly. "I don't know how I'll be."

I took in the other nipple and after a while said, "I'll worry about that."

His cock was hard, it pointed up in the air from his own lap. I took it in my hand and could feel the dampness. He sighed above me, and willingly let my hands roam over his ass, shifting slightly to let my palms cup one of his cheeks.

Eventually I led him to the bedroom. I put him down on the mattress and stripped. Our mouths met one another, then they each traveled over the other's body. Cocks, balls, chests and stomachs were all licked and tasted. I eventually fucked him. His strong arms embraced me; the mammoth biceps pressed against my shoulders. "Daddy, fuck your little boy, fuck him hard."

I did. I came strangely and forcibly and ecstatically. He jerked himself off while my ebbing cock stayed in his ass. Soon a puddle of little boy cum splashed onto my belly.

The weekend was too short. There wasn't time to rebuild. Dinners were pleasant, sex was good. The conversation was what he needed most; the reaffirmation was essential.

He was unsure of himself. He wasn't looking for answers—he knew there were none. But he needed attention. He needed to talk and to experience someone hearing him, to speak intelligent words and know someone valued them.

He also needed attention paid to his body. It was not a substitute for his self-worth, but he wanted to know he could still attract a man with it. Would someone be proud of it?

I took him to a dance bar one night. He moved gracefully with that special style of a New Yorker who's taken dancing to a place near professional. I watched him move on the floor and turned myself on with the sight of his body and the knowledge that it was mine for this time.

Once, when he had come off the floor to rest, I ran a hand over the sweat-covered arms and told him to take his shirt off when he went back. "No one else has," he objected. I told him again.

When he went out to the floor with a friend of mine he looked back at me and stared for a second. As his torso moved luxuriously with the sounds he stripped off his shirt and revealed the chest that had given me such pleasure. A stranger's hand came out and had to touch it. Another stranger came up to me and asked if I knew that man.

The other dancers watched his half-naked physique with more than appreciation, perhaps with envy. His motions were even more dramatic now as his audience had become more obvious.

Soon he was back with me and even more sweat poured off his skin. I wiped it with my palm and felt its wet and smelled its perfume. "You're beautiful."

He kissed me.

That night I fucked him again. I wanted every inch of his body to touch mine. "Please, Daddy, please…" he whispered.

The next and last morning I again watched him shower

from my seat in the next room. We talked while I played the voyeur to his nakedness.

Later we sat and had coffee. The cloud of his return to New York was taking away his attention. Just as the fantasy of the Mineshaft had come to an end so was the breathing space of this trip to Maine. I was, for a while, losing him. He sensed it and apologized. I waved it away. "It's fine. It's fine."

I drove him to the airport and made sure his reservations were there. He secured his ticket and we said our good-byes.

I went home and read the Sunday papers. Later that night I thought about him and of his body. But the words came more strongly, "Daddy, tell me everything will be all right."

ESCALATION

Oh yeah!

That's the best way to describe what it feels like. When you're standing across a barroom or on the opposite side of a street, or you're at a party or in the subway. It makes a tingle spread in your groin, a sensation that grows from anticipation. It calms your nerves and makes you stand ramrod stiff, not from fear but from some primeval knowledge that sex is going to happen.

It's not what goes on when you *hope* sex will happen or when you're *trying* to make it happen or when you *need* sex to happen. *Oh yeah!* happens when *sex is going* to happen.

I felt it that night at the bar in Philadelphia. It only took one look from me and one more back to him. It was set. The friend I had come with blended into the background and the man I had been studying for an hour disappeared from my sight.

The new one I had just swapped signals with had been at the same meeting I had attended earlier in the day. He had been the one man in the whole convention that I had really wanted.

Now he was giving me a cool but constant stare across the short distance. It was unmistakable.

He wasn't as tall as I, but hardly short. He had close-cropped hair and a mandatory moustache. He would have been skinny but the chest muscles were too broad and the two pectorals pressed nicely against his t-shirt.

He knew a secret too often forgotten in the gay world: loose-fitting clothes can reveal more than tight ones. His jeans hung freely from his waist. I saw what was bulged up inside the folds and I remembered a t-shirt that just had become popular: "I'm not a size queen, but I can be impressed."

It was supposed to be a leather bar, though I wouldn't have given it many medals. Still, attempts were being made by some of the patrons to give off that image. He wasn't buying into it. He had none of the apparent affectations that some use to cement their identity with a place like this one. He was listening to the music and his body was moving with smooth undulating motions to keep in time with the beat. He wasn't dancing; that would have been verboten and he probably knew it; he was just comfortably moving with the sounds.

His hips made liquid moves and his chest and arms kept them subtle company. But once he had locked his eyes on mine his face was frozen.

I knew I was going to fuck him.

That was what it was all about. Years of practice, the stripping away of guilt and fear were to let us stand there and know that. One man does it to be soothed, another as a physical gift, another as an experiment. The trick was to admit you wanted it. I wanted to fuck him, and he wanted me to fuck him. We were both graduates. We both knew it.

The idea has been to meet naked and ready, hot and heavy. Take what you want and just make sure you give something heavy back in return. Want to spend the night together, strangers in a strange city?

Oh yeah!

So I walked over. The usual preliminaries weren't necessary—our eyes had made that clear enough. I just stood beside him. We talked about the convention, then moved onto some different small talk. Where was I from? Maine. And him? Indiana.

Damn the disease. We both studied one another and I could sense each of us gauging the risk. It wasn't a bad one. Two healthy looking men; two "healthy" states. I felt a momentary guilt as I wondered what I would have done if he had been from New York or California. But he wasn't, so I didn't ponder it too long. I assumed he went through the same kind of thing, and we kept talking.

He did not, however, stop moving. The physical response to the music was constant. Where had he been earlier, I asked. "I tried to go dancing, but the places people told me about weren't right." He paused, looked at me coolly, "I wanted a masculine place, a male experience. I like women, don't get me wrong, but I wanted to be with men. I couldn't find that tonight."

He was amused by the isolation of where I lived—"You must be the only person I ever met from Maine," he had said—but it was clear he was less used to the big city faggots that littered the convention than I was.

The sexual sensations between us were heavy, thick in the air. It was easy to say, "Mind if I seduce you?"

He smiled broadly, "You mean before I seduce you?"

We were both from out of town. He was sharing a hotel room with someone else; I was staying with friends on a mattress on the floor. I think we would have done it in the lobby if it had been necessary, though, and the idea of a mattress on the floor wasn't an issue at all.

We took a cab; when we arrived everyone else had already gone to sleep. We had been talking comfortably and there wasn't much more to say so I found a couple of candles and lit them. It was a slight element of the romantic in the middle of the mundane, but the warm glow seemed to overtake the room and soften the idea of crashing on the floor in a stranger's house.

We didn't undress right away, we just laid down on the mattress and his head rested on my shoulder. We kissed. He did it well. He did everything well, I realized, as his one leg came up and looped over my waist. There wasn't the need to strip right away and go at it; there was an agreement that the foreplay should be pleasurable. It was.

My hands slid up underneath his t-shirt and found hard nubs on the nearly hairless chest. The nipples rose up high when they erected. The little sighs let me know he wanted my fingers just where they were. They stayed there.

I lifted the shirt high enough to let my tongue lick one nipple. More sounds. My teeth nipped at it. He pushed his chest forward as though he wanted more pressure. He got a lot more.

Through a squirming motion he let me know he was feeling the sensations intensely, but as much as he would twist and manipulate his own body it was also clear he didn't want me to stop. It was as if his nipples were locked into place even if the rest of him had to move.

It all went on long enough that I was surprised, eventually, that we hadn't undressed. I could feel his cock hard against my stomach. My own was just as hard and the sense of its entrapment in my clothes was delicious. I decided to enjoy all this. My mouth moved back and forth, my teeth moved at will between little gnaws and occasional bites hard enough to bring a guttural sound from him. The first time he tried to resist I held his hands tightly. After that he never tried to move them again. The acceptance of his position was a subtle but erotic conquest.

We stopped. Easily, quickly. I just rolled over and left him there. He brought his arms down and we silently lit cigarettes and smoked in the dark. We talked, going beyond the superficialities of where we lived to explore more about who we were and where we had come from. There were nice little physical touches in there, mine and his both. We had a kind of ease that usually doesn't happen until two men have known one another for a long time. I didn't think about it much.

When the cigarettes were gone, we started again. I slid my hand down his jeans this time, letting my mouth do all the work on his chest. His ass was covered with a thick coating of hair that was unexpected after the smoothness of his upper torso. It actually felt furry. I moved my hand to undo his buttons and to let the jeans move down over his hips. His cock was just as big as I had thought it might be. I was as impressed as I had expected to be.

"What's a little boy like you doing with a thing like that?"

"Is that what I am? A little boy?" There was a severity in his question. He didn't like the idea one bit. Okay, I thought, no games. I kissed him as an answer.

I moved on top of him. He let me climb up, then wrapped

his legs around the outside of mine. If I had ever doubted that I would fuck him the doubt left at that moment with that reaction of his limbs. He was opening himself up to my invasion.

We kept on going as though we were two high school kids at the drive-in. Kissing, hands searching, bodies moving to grind our pelvises together, I finally lifted my head up and smiled down at him, "I gotta fuck you."

He smiled. "It can be arranged."

There was a silent agreement to stop for a minute and undress. We did it quickly and effectively. When we were both naked and he slid back underneath me, the length of our bodies met flesh to flesh. It was a good sensation. The bushes of our crotches meshed their hair together. Once more his legs lifted up for me and my hard cock went below and pressed against the cheeks of his ass. His pushed against my belly and left a warm tubular impression on my skin.

There were moments when we would stop kissing and look at one another. I should have recognized them—maybe I could have forestalled things. But I didn't. Men don't often allow those looks to happen right away, they usually go off into some dream world. They don't want to study your face because it could distract from their fantasies. They want you to be something or someone other than who you are. To study you is to take in more reality than they want to deal with.

But we studied one another a lot, right from the start. I thought—at least I thought this at first—that I was taking in more of his features. His nose was prominent. He had beautiful eyes. His skin was smooth with no sign of blemish now or ever before. His lips were rounded and nicely colored. His chin was strong. His smile created a glittering look. It was almost mischievous, a conspiratorial appearance that would take over as though he were laughing with me about a shared secret.

A moment of reality: we needed lubricant. I went to search my hosts' bathroom for something, delighting in the way my erection waved in the air as I walked down the corridor. When I returned he was smoking again. I lit up and laid down beside him. He nestled closer, his smaller body resting nicely against mine.

The bottle of lubricant which was so obviously ready for use wasn't any kind of barrier to our conversation. He had read something; I had talked to somebody. The knowledge that we were going to fuck was just a part of it all. So many other times and places, a man would have had to be dirty-talking if he were in a place like this one, psyching himself up for it or trying to make it more immediately erotic. Not us, not that night. We were together. Talking was part of it, just as fucking was.

When we were done smoking and the cigarettes were extinguished I rolled back on top of him. My cock, momentarily rested, sprung back up hard and found its niche in the cleft of his ass. The hair that covered his buttocks was matched by a thick layer on his legs. I commented on how little hair there was over his waist, how much beneath it. He had obviously heard it before and just shrugged; it was the body he had and that was that.

I greased the length of my cock and placed some of the stuff up his warm hole. It felt good, wet and comfortable to have my finger up there. His mouth opened with a slight hiss, not to complain but to convey relief to have the inner contact.

His legs willingly came up over my shoulders and I let my cock slide in. Kisses. Arms around chests. Hips against hips.

Long, long thrusts, each matched by a slow, slow pulling back, pulling back so far that I could almost feel my cock escape. Whenever that threatened his arms would clasp me harder and his sphincter would contract as though he were anxious for me to stay, almost frightened I would leave him.

It became an exercise in endurance. We started with me on top, we moved till we were on our sides where it was more comfortable and our bodies seemed better prepared to take the relaxed fucking. My hands would work his chest, grip his cock and balls and smooth the skin on his back. Long, long thrusts, my cock encased in his ass, warm and protected, then coming so far out that I could feel the evening air on the shaft.

We would change tempo. I'd suddenly push him back, forcing out that hiss of surprise again and I'd crash into him with hard, quick plunges that brought a sharp breath each time my pelvis slammed his hips. I'd bring myself so close to orgasm that I'd suddenly have to stop and I'd just lie there on top of him, clenching my teeth, willing the orgasm to go away, wanting this to last.

He never stopped me.

I took myself up to the peak and nearly over the edge a number of times. Sometimes with slams, more often with the sensual, careful, caring motions. We rolled over the floor like two experienced athletes. Wordlessly we were asking each other, "Done it this way? Felt that before? Want to try this one?"

Finally I moved out of him and got the first real protest. I closed it off with a kiss and let our arms relax. "I have to rest. I don't want to end it too quickly."

He replied with the conspiratorial smile again. I had said the right thing.

More talk. Another cigarette. More touching.

Then I was erect once more. I was inside him again; I was protected by the moist channels of his ass again. It was a momentary obsession to be doing it. I thought of other sexual things as well. I wanted to pull out of him and move him onto his stomach. I wanted to play with his ass. I wanted him to feel hard wallops on his naked butt. It hadn't been prepared for, though. We had met in a leather bar of sorts, but that was all. The slight motions of holding his hands over his head hadn't been used to communicate anything heavier. I had only asked to fuck him. He was with me to get fucked.

I was content to watch my cock invading him, to watch his hand move on his own cock and I let my mouth bite his closer nipple and I felt the protection of his ass and…I shot. I shot with all the energy that had been pent up for so long and my blood raced through all of me, but especially my cock. Loud noises came unconsciously from my throat.

His hand sped up and soon, remarkably soon, there was the explosion of his own cum on his belly, the white fluid beaded on his skin. I reached down, still inside him, and I spread it out over the hair above his crotch. The stuff was thick and almost pasty. We looked at each other; he smiled his elfin smile. We kissed.

I hated to have my cock taken out of his ass, but the first lights of dawn were coming through the window. We had to sleep. Damned sleep. We laid side by side and I watched him close his eyes and fall easily away from me while my hands roamed unhindered on his smooth skin.

We were awakened in the morning by the sounds of the household. I don't remember who woke first. My usual opening grouchiness melted in front of his immediate smile and the quick kiss. Unbelievably my cock was already hard again. I forced him back down on the mattress and climbed up once more. "I gotta fuck you again," I said. But I could see the distraction in his face. There was a conference session starting soon. I didn't push the issue. "There's an hour and a half lunch break, your hotel room?"

He looked relieved. "Sure." The relief, I understood, came because if I had insisted he would have stayed. He would have let me fuck him again if I had insisted. I felt like kicking myself for letting him go that way; I could have had him again, right then. I tried to convince myself that I was accepting his obligations as a rational adult should. My cock told me I was a fool.

He and I walked to the convention hotel. The people were gathered and all the ones who thought the world's future was being decided were running around making themselves feel important. I drank coffee in the anteroom while he rushed upstairs and quickly showered and changed. When he came down he stopped briefly to touch me and smile, then I watched him as he went to his seat and greeted a couple acquaintances and shook a few new hands.

I finally went inside and took the chair beside him. He was intent on the speaker's words. I was intent on his ass. He was leaning forward. His posture made his jeans pucker in the back. He had put on a pair of underpants and I could look down the back of his slacks and see the elastic band and the thin line of exposed skin. I wanted desperately to put my hand down there.

I used my self-control and then damned myself for it. I couldn't be bothered with the speaker. I had heard it before and it wasn't going to change my life or anyone else's. I tried to think about other things, but the sense of him was too strong.

I kept going back to the night before. I got hard. I stole more glances at that line of elastic that peeked at me and at the skin that made him look so hairless even though I knew his buttocks were fully coated.

I wondered more about him. I fantasized about taking him right there, just reaching over and moving him across my lap, pulling down those offensive jeans and the underwear that covered his bottom. I dreamt about holding his hands behind his back and slapping his ass, wondering what it would feel like to give that to him, how my hand would sting and his skin respond.

I relished the memory of his body. His stomach had been tight, almost to that place where you could have seen the horizontal lines of muscles. His legs were handsomely proportioned, his thighs thick and hard, his calves firm and rounded. His arms were masculine and had the curves of a man's muscles. His ass, I remembered with my hard on pulsing, had been a surprise. It wasn't soft, certainly not feminine, but it had been much less hard than the rest of him. It had been like a fur-covered pillow. I wondered what it would be like to fuck him from behind, to fuck him in a position that would let me feel that cushion of a furry pillow while I rested on him, my cock inside him.

I nearly went away to beat off. But I comforted myself that we'd go and fuck at lunch time. It wouldn't be long.

There was something erotic about that idea, the idea of running to his room upstairs and doing it while the rest of the convention kept up its dreary business over restaurant tables. Perhaps it came from the secretiveness or the furtiveness. Whatever, I liked the concept.

The time passed. I would wander occasionally, sometimes when the sight of his ass got me too strongly, sometimes when the speakers' words became too oppressive. I'd go and read a newspaper, or go talk to someone in the lobby. But I would always come back and he'd be there, seldom moving much.

As the noon hour approached I realized that these fools weren't keeping up with their schedule. The precious lunch hour started to melt away as motions were presented and voted on and ridiculous debates about nothing important took place. Nothing that was important compared to him.

When they finally did break it was only a half-hour recess. He looked at me and I could see that it wasn't going to work. The disappointment was intense; I didn't recognize just how intense it felt to me. I would later. We shrugged and went to lunch with another person. It was pleasant and we all entertained one another, and I comforted myself with the feeling that there was always the afternoon.

The meeting was supposed to be over about three. I didn't need to leave Philadelphia until eight, and he wasn't departing till the next day. Three to eight. Five hours. More than we had spent last night. It'd do. I tried to calm my cock. "You're going to be fine," I tried to reassure it. "You're going to be taken care of."

The meeting droned on, and on. Into the late afternoon. I tried to maintain my calm. But there was this man sitting beside me and as soon as this fiasco was over I was going to get to fuck him and these idiots were talking about amendments to a constitution of an organization no one besides the group gathered gave a shit about or had ever heard of before. Where was their sense of priority!? He sat calmly through it, a counterpoise to my anxiety. I felt calmed by his ease. I wondered why his composure didn't bother me.

Eventually the situation got to me—not him, but the waiting for him. I started passing little notes. He seemed to find it amusing—not so much my notes but my need to break in as though I were jealous for his attention. Out of desperation I finally wrote, "Are we going to get more time together?"

He whispered an answer, "Fifteen minutes."

"*What!*"

"Shhhh!" the man next to me complained.

"In fifteen minutes we'll leave," he smiled.

That's when I should have known. When I was willing to regress to passing notes as though I were in junior high school and I was begging him to go and fuck, I should have known.

It really was coming to an end. We left the meeting only a little before the closing minutes. I tried to be cool. We talked about the day's events and I told myself that these things could be important if you hadn't been to many, and he hadn't.

We rode the elevator up to his floor and found his room. It was like any other hotel chain in the country: two double beds, a big bath, loud-colored patterns on the spreads, bland wall coverings with permanently attached fixtures, a vague view of a city skyline. His roommate was there getting ready for a party. Then he decided he wanted a fresh shower. Then he decided he'd smoke a cigarette with us. Then he decided he'd have another. I thought I'd decide to throw him out the nineteenth floor window.

There was a scheming look on my companion's face when he finally watched his roommate leave, as though it had amused him to watch my politeness as it had merged with my discomfort and anxiousness.

When the door did finally close we dove onto the bed. Arms went around each other, my hands roved back to his nipples. I knew they must be sore and sensitive after the last night, and they obviously were, but the touch on them made him squirm with clear and distinct delight.

He broke off eventually and stood up, needing to go into the bathroom. "You know, I really wanted to hit your ass last night." He froze. He looked back and grinned more broadly than ever before. "You should have."

He rejoined me in the bed in a few minutes. We were both naked now, horny and ready and our cocks were hard and our balls were pulled up in their sacs. No matter that the kiss was as sensuous as before, a new topic had been broached and there was a wanton manner in our embrace now.

I could sense it whenever my hands roamed over his skin. Now he wasn't just enjoying the exploration; he was waiting for the slap, the feel of my palm. I could sense his wondering where and when it would come.

I had felt no hesitation about holding his hands above his head last night, nor about chewing on his tits. But now I didn't waver about the force I used. I took his wrists with a hard grasp and lifted them up. My mouth chewed on his chest without wavering, without wondering if he wanted it, without any attempt at modulation.

His body reacted sharply. It moved more quickly and more forcibly as though it too had been given some permission that hadn't been received last night.

It didn't hesitate when I rolled him over, pressing myself against his back and lifting up his ass. He moaned loudly with anticipation as I ran my palm over his hairy buttocks. When I finally did slap him—hard—he erupted in a vehement movement that was close to violence. His vocal response became a scream that he muffled in the pillow. I slapped him again and then watched the redness leave its transitory tattoo on his ass. I wanted to go on but I couldn't read his signals clearly now; that intense reaction could have been joy, or it could have been the beginning of hatred. With someone else at a different time I might have progressed, not caring which, but not this encounter. Not with him.

I stopped. I climbed up and lubricated my cock, leaving him face down. I slipped it in and started to pump. His legs spread apart, his arms reached up to the headboard and grasped a tight hold. He lifted his ass up to greet me.

The stress he put his body under made him look much more muscular. His head was still buried in the pillow and I could hear him plead, "Fuck me. Fuck that ass." Without his mouth and the touch of his hand he became nameless. For a moment of anonymity he was every man I ever wanted to fuck. Masculine in appearance, submissive in demeanor, muscular in build…he was as beautiful as any man could be in that namelessness.

I fucked him as hard as I could. If it was possible, I was fucking him with more and harder and quicker strokes than I had last night. I lifted myself up on my hands and knees and left only my cock in his ass as our physical contact. I refused to come, he tried to coax me with practiced motions and consciously maintained clenchings of his hole. I refused to come.

The eroticism didn't ebb when I pulled out. I quickly brought him back to face me and wrapped my arms around him. I brought him back from anonymity with my kisses and his arms accepted me with tight embraces. Our bodies met and our sweat mingled on our chests.

No passion was subdued by the change; our cocks were still hard. But our eyes met now. We recognized one another.

We spent a long lazy time pleasuring one another. We alternated how we each did it. I would chew, bite and push; he responded by gently licking, quickly caressing and constantly returning his head to a slightly subdued position against my chest or in the nook of my neck.

Just as before we went on for hours. I forgot the clock. We took a break. We talked. We fucked more, sometimes with violent passion, sometimes with gentle seduction.

I found myself exploring his body more quietly. I found little things that pleased me greatly. With the smooth skin above his waist uncovered by hair, that growth under his arms took on a great power, it became a fetish. I smelt it, licked it, lifting his arms up to keep him from barring my entry.

The whole thing broke when his roommate knocked on the door. I sprawled away from him and heard them talk. "Five minutes," he shrugged when he came back to the bed. "He's got to get back to change clothes again. It's his room too. I can't stop him." There wasn't a need to explain. But just five minutes to end all this?

I suddenly liked the idea. I pulled him down and drove my already greased cock into him. I pulled him up by one of the cheeks of his ass and started to fuck him, using the hold on his buttock to drive him in as I thrust at him. I rocked him on the mattress, setting up a rhythm so the springing surface only helped increase the force. He never resisted; he seemed to enjoy the suddenness of it. The moans were all pleasure. He was facing me this time and the kisses I received were all appreciative.

I came in a quick few minutes and exploded in him, arching my back with the anguish of the consummation of all those hours. I collapsed on top of him; my smell was strong and my breathing was harsh.

He just smiled. He just smiled and kissed the top of my head as he let his lips run lightly over my neck.

By the time the roommate returned we were under the covers. There was some small talk. The roommate left us soon and we showered. We made out under the spray. I teased him about his sensitive tits. "You'll feel those later. That's good. I like being remembered." He laughed.

I tried to get out of going. I called New York to see if I could cancel my appointment and spend the night there in Philadelphia with him; he wasn't returning to Indiana till the next day. I couldn't make my connection and knew my own responsibilities dictated I leave, just as his had kept us in the meeting all day.

The train I had to take wasn't leaving for another forty-five minutes, so I asked him to come to the station with me. We could at least have a drink and prolong everything as much as possible. Maybe I could try to call New York again. He started to agree and then suddenly stopped collecting his clothes and shook his head. No. It'd be silly. I agreed and felt sad—and then it struck me.

Oh no!

That's the best way to describe what it feels like. When you're standing in a room and a heavy sensation comes over you that means you're vulnerable. It makes you have to decide not to stand stiffly and protectively and it comes from fear that this is too much, or might be too much, or—even worse—might not be enough.

We said good-bye. I walked out of the hotel and caught a cab. I mindlessly watched the driver's route to the train station. I climbed on board a Metroliner and thought all the way to New York.

I had once been able to exchange my body without much thought or expectation. But the passing of strangers through my bed—even if they came and went with a memory of pleasure—had ceased to be desirable, at least it had ceased being desirable as the only way people moved through my bed. I had spent years learning to let individuals linger, to allow myself to savor known bodies and known emotions. There were friends who shared my beds, and playful playmates, and there had been lovers.

But now—by choice—I was alone. And I had no conscious idea that I had chosen to have these emotions sweep over me, not when they were brought on by a stranger during one weekend.

I could leave this man. It's easily done. I wouldn't write; I wouldn't respond if he did; I would leave the sex isolated, just as I had learned to do so well so long ago. If he intruded in my thoughts, I would dismiss him.

Oh no!

All the things happened that are just as predictable as the other set.

I wrote a letter as soon as I got home a week later. I tried to make it light, I hoped the hints of need and want were well cloaked. There was just information and a little sentence about wanting to go on. I waited too anxiously for a reply and I was too relieved to see the answer when it was sitting in my post office box. I read it, looking for the signal. I found it. "I too would like to see the relationship continue in any possible form."

So the letters began. At first they were in a careful letter/response/letter/response sequence. Then, one day, there was the next step. I had waited for it. It was a simple card. He had been someplace and it had reminded him of me. It was a familiar escalation.

I coaxed him to write more, reveal more. I suppose I wanted him to share my sense of vulnerability. He wasn't resistant, but there were areas that he skimmed or there would be sudden revelations that changed the meaning of everything that had come before.

I wanted his opinion of the sex. He wrote: "I couldn't make you stop. I felt as if I needed to let you enjoy me and I wanted you to know that even if it hurt I accepted it, even wanted it."

In the next letter he talked about a man he had mentioned. They had met. It had been powerful enough to demand a second visit even though they lived thousands of miles apart. He told me: "We met and we shared that sort of immediate infatuation that seems to be a rarity in my life. That it happens so infrequently doesn't bother me. When he left the first time I found it hard to believe that I actually hurt because he was going away. It all seemed so irrational to me."

There is a quote I have written on a note card and placed over my desk. It's from Marguerite Yourcenar's *Fires:*

> It is not a question of sublimation, which is itself a very unfortunate term and one that insults the body, but a dark perception that love for a particular person, so poignant, is

> often only a beautiful fleeting accident, less real in a way than the predispositions and choices that preceded it and that will follow it.

I studied the quote again. What were my predispositions? Was I just lonely at this moment? Was I just clinging to a sexual moment that would best be left alone? Was my need for solitude too great to be broken? Was that, perhaps, why the passions of my sexuality and my emotions came so violently—because the rest of me was so pacific?

Did I want this? Infatuation is like a thunderstorm to me, a violent wind that comes into my life and swirls ideas and emotions around but then leaves them as debris not only not helping me to put them back together again, but having accomplished nothing, really, by their disruption. I have traveled foolishly for infatuation. I have given up things and feelings too easily without care to where they were being sent and without the ability to retrieve them.

Sexual passions, somehow different, can leave me charged with electrical energy and with a sense that the sheer excitement of it all had made everything valuable as an experience.

Sexual pleasure is something that, as an autonomous man, I have been able to share with other men. Friends, buddies and I have given each other our bodies as gifts. Those I have learned to accept graciously.

And I have been in love.

The intensity of this man from Indiana left me unsure what had happened. Had I read too much into the simple act of passion? Would I destroy needlessly the friendship that could come from sexual pleasure?

I focused on the time we had spent and realized how much everything was based on there having been too little of it. It was as though our probing of one another had been inconclusive. I couldn't discern if this was love, infatuation or delusion—or what kind of mixture of all three.

Another letter: "You remarked that there seems to be an 'incompleteness' involved in this relationship and I agree. For whatever reasons I want to be available to you."

I became angry at my motivations. I wanted to fly to Indiana and destroy this all. I wanted to see him at home, watch him be unreasonable about something, observe him be careless. I wanted to witness my right to leave and return to myself.

I became frightened by my inability to do it. I could not hide from myself any more, even now when I wanted to. I had done that and it hadn't worked and I wouldn't attempt it again. So, if I did go to Indiana, I would only be risking more of this exposure to these emotions that were not ever going to be rational.

I talked to a friend. "Isn't that what it's all about?" he responded.

A last letter arrived yesterday: "I need to be with you again, as soon as it's possible."

Oh no!

Yes.

EPILOGUE
ON WRITING PORNOGRAPHY

Many people ask how I began writing sexual fiction, how I go about doing it, and to what extent it's autobiographical. They ask in a way that's both shy and sly: shy because these people are talking about sex and sly because they seem to think they've "caught" me writing about it.

However much they reveal their intrigue about pornography and its creation, they almost always try to draw back the veil across their own faces. They attempt to deny any serious interest; most often that's done with a quick dismissive statement to me: "When are you going to do some real writing?"

I usually find these responses amusing; they're only occasionally even annoying. What will exasperate me are those literary people who express surprise that I "still" write pornography. These are usually those who think erotic fiction is a stage one might have to go through—probably for financial reasons—rather than any kind of goal a writer might ever aspire to. They seem to think that anyone who writes political essays, news journalism and even nonsexual novels shouldn't be involved in this kind of thing any more.

They certainly seem to think that the least I should do is move from their concept of "pornography" towards something they would label "erotica." I find the creation of this dichotomy between types of sexual fiction to be silly, as if these critics would like to cover the smell of bodily fluids with a goodly dose of perfume. I personally don't like to have sex with perfumed men so my descriptions will have to stay where my narration pays attention to physical odors.

Yet I have to admit that I had my own prejudices about pornography before I began to write it five years ago. In fact it was those preconceptions that allowed me to write it in the first place. But once I started writing sexual fiction I learned many things quickly. They all combined to alter how I envisioned sexual fiction—not just what I was writing, but what I read.

I have written almost every form of pornography. I have had almost every conceivable motivation for doing it at one time or another. All this is relevant here because I consider that thread of my writing that's made up of sexual fiction to have reached a certain point with the stories in this volume.

Because this volume does define a stage in my writing, I'd like to describe what I've gone through to reach this place. I can satisfy that self-indulgence since it apparently interests so many readers—at least it would seem so from all those questions I'm asked. This of course is the author's favorite position—to want to write what people say they want to read.

Writing isn't an easy occupation, certainly not in the beginning. It often appears to be, and I certainly thought it should be. I caught myself again and again saying, "I could do that." Thing was, I couldn't. Whenever I'd sit down and attempt to write, especially fiction, I would be instantly paralyzed.

The problems were self-inflicted. For one thing I thought anything that came out of my typewriter should be of high literary quality on the first draft; anything less was unacceptable, and that meant everything I did was unacceptable.

But writing for gay magazines lifted some of these burdens, or so it seemed at first. It would only be writing about sex, I thought; it would only be pornography. If I chose I could hide behind a pseudonym. With little more thought than that I began. It might have been that I would only have done a story or two if *Drummer* hadn't been my first publishing contact.

Usually the editors of gay magazines have no time for editing in any real sense of the word. It's not a question of callousness on their part, nor necessarily of indifference. They are simply understaffed. The most response a writer can hope for is a request for a rewrite if something shows a lot of promise. *Drummer* can be quite different. Its editor—John Rowberry for most of the time I have published there—and its publisher John Embry have a more directive sense of their magazine and what should be in it.

My first submission was a short story which they thought worked well enough that they asked me to use it as the first chapter for a novel. If I would write it, they would serialize it. That first short story became *Mr. Benson,* now a book, and it altered what I could do in many ways.

But while *Mr. Benson* was being written there were numerous other articles and stories that *Drummer* wanted. Their interest in me was heightened because I was then living in New York and could fill their need for more national editorial content than they were able to produce solely from their San Francisco base.

What this essentially meant was that I could avoid one of the most discouraging things a writer has to go through: finding someone interested in publishing his or her work. The results were mixed, but the reception remained warm and I continued.

The first thing that happened was that I altered the way I was looking at the world. I was constantly striving to find something new to write about and my day-to-day existence was the best place for me to investigate. Everything became sexual; there was no situation where I couldn't find the setting for one of these pieces *Drummer* wanted. I'd walk into a deli and look at it as a potential site for an orgy. Every man I met was a possible character for future use. No piece of clothing could be dismissed until it had been examined as a fetish for some plot.

Now, I was hardly a sexual innocent at this point. Far from it: like many other young men from working-class towns I had used hustling the nearest big city Greyhound terminal as a way to come out. But for as much action as I may have taken part in, there had been little available that helped me think about sex.

I had gone on to become actively involved in gay liberation but—especially during the time I was significantly part of that movement—it didn't want to deal with sex directly. If anything, the movement was anti-sexual. Everyone was so worried that straights would see us as people consumed with a vast orgasmic drive that we always tried to deny that the possibility even existed.

I had even tried to cope with the sexual reality of the world by entering a graduate program in human sexuality. But since the context was a state university worried about funding from a conservative legislature, the program didn't progress any further, really, than the rest of society. True, it was a "scientific" context and therefore didn't cloak sex with layers of romance and relational obligation, but it didn't seem to really work to have academia as the vehicle for examining this strange phenomenon's power and position in our lives. Lectures and panel discussions, sociological studies and psychological evaluation didn't always clarify very much. The mysteries of sex remained intact, more often than not, and their power to create misery and celebration even further obscured.

These were very strange times for me.

But what I discovered by writing about sex for *Drummer* was exciting. I began to encounter my own blocks to my own sexuality and my own capability for sexual intimacy. Why had I denied certain potentials? What did I think would happen to me if I took another step, went to a certain place, experienced a new act? Writing fiction let me look at those situations.

I experience writing pornography in precisely the same way I expect people who read pornography do—as an examination of possibilities and potentials. Since I had freed myself from any literary restraints other than the telling of a good story, I could address myself to my own discoveries.

I think many of those stories had a glee about them. I know I had that sense of fun while doing the writing. I felt as though I were saying to a whole group of people, "Come and look at this one. You won't believe what I've done this time!"

Then three things happened in quick succession. My articles

and stories began to appear on the newsstand. (Most people don't realize that there's a lag of many months between writing and publication.) It is difficult to explain just how different it is to see one's words in printed form rather than typewritten on paper; the impact can be amazing. While I was facing this dilemma I also had to face another that was utterly unexpected: people not only read what I wrote, they wanted to talk about it, they wrote letters, they stopped me on the street. Finally, while I was still reeling from these stuns, *Mr. Benson*'s serialization began.

I've never fully understood just why *Mr. Benson* became quite so popular. There were fan clubs, letter, and t-shirts. Some raw nerve had been struck. This was totally unanticipated. When I had finished the book the publisher called one day and asked what name I wanted to use with it. I simply went along with his assumption that I should take a pseudonym. Why use my real name? No one was going to notice the author anyway. But in fact they did. *Drummer,* and now other magazines, wanted more articles and more fiction from me. I had earned a new identity: pornographer.

I didn't duck this label. On the contrary, I wrote more and I began to photograph male nudes as well—a great enjoyment. I still thought I was only trying to tell a story, often one inspired by a specific photographic image or a particular erotic memory. But as the pages mounted I couldn't help but see that there were certain themes which ran through most of what I did.

There was the sense of exploration that I've commented on. Also a perception of sex as a cathartic experience. Most of all, there was an implicit judgment that to avoid a sexual experience was to lose an opportunity for a whole range of personal investigations that went far beyond a genital experience. I realized that sex, for me, never happened in a vacuum: it was always something that could alter a person's perceptions of the world and even his position within it.

I also learned something important about myself as a writer. While I don't think I indulged in a self-deception of myself as a member of any literati, I realized that the responses I was getting from readers were making me take much of my writing more seriously.

The fact that I began my writing with *Drummer* had a great deal to do with this. More than any other gay magazine *Drummer* knows precisely to whom it's directed. There is a very specific audience and that audience cares tremendously about what's in the magazine's pages. There is a sense of unity about *Drummer* that few publications have; perhaps only a periodical like the *New Yorker* is comparable, for instance in the way advertising copy is as much an integral part of the final package as the fiction and editorial reportage.

Because I had read *Drummer* for years before I wrote for it, and because I identified myself as one of its readers, I suppose I had an intrinsic sense of who the rest of the readers were, how they would see things, what they would like to hear and how to use what words to communicate what emotions to them.

I had begun by writing fiction that was heavily fantasy-laden. Certainly that's true with *Mr. Benson*. Increasingly I wrote things that people could see as possibilities for themselves. The fantasy became less and less important. Instead a constant return to looking at what really happened in gay life and what could be made out of it took over, emotionally and sexually. If I hadn't liked the people who read gay magazines and gay books in general I might never have seen that pornography holds a rather unique place as a vernacular literature in the gay world, more so than elsewhere.

It was at about this time that I picked a guide for myself. Like most other people, I had used pornography in one way or another since I had begun to be sexual. As I realized that some people separated out my own work and that of some other writers such as T. R. Witomski and Dennis Schuetz, I remembered that certain work I had read had made a great impact on me, certainly greater than what I usually expected to receive from sexual writing.

I retraced my reading and discovered that most of the books and stories that had stood out so starkly from the rest of the erotic fiction I had known had been written by one person, Samuel Steward. This was the man who had published the Phil Andros novels, which are now having such a deserved rebirth in new publication. I went on to discover a lot more about him and his life and even made what I've always called a "little pilgrimage" to meet Steward in California.

Steward and his career helped me put myself and my work into a context. He certainly ripped away any shreds of self-deprecation I might have still had about being an erotic writer. His forays into sexual fiction hadn't defined him in any constraining manner and he—after all, he was a protégé of Gertrude Stein's—felt free to move back and forth between pornography and any other kind of writing he chose to do.

My investigation of Steward's work was no minor inquiry. I started work on a biography of him, a project short-circuited only by the publication of his own autobiography. Most of the lessons I learned from Steward were things I already had begun to have a grip on, but my awareness of them became more conscious, and the decision to use certain perceptions and to include certain kinds of information were given a more solid foundation because of his example.

I can define some specifics; for one thing, there is nothing wrong with writing something that is essentially meant to be just an entertainment. (There sometimes seems to be some prejudice that writing should be always *meaningful* and often difficult; this is not dissimilar to the view that medicine should taste bad, I suppose.) Sex is first and foremost fun. Sex is desired and desirable. If these rules are broken, it's a sure sign someone's being dishonest, misusing sex or someone else, or in some other way, somebody is mixing up the works. Still, it's always true that sex seldom happens alone; it produces emotions and it flows from emotions.

There's still another statement to be made that had great importance to Steward: writing about sex is one of the best ways possible to inform the gay world about itself, including issues with which it should be concerned and potential problems it might face.

When Steward and a few other gay writers began their publishing careers—in terms of *gay writing*—they were limited to sexual themes because their only hope for publication was sleazy pornographic publishing houses. Only by meeting the erotic requirements of those houses could a writer like Sam Steward inform his readers about disease and its spread, the danger of police entrapment, the locales of gay gathering places, and more.

There is still another level where Steward's point of view informed me about my own values. When we talked and wrote about our readers it was very apparent that he also actively liked the gay men who would read our writing. At one level it might seem a minor point, but it became increasingly relevant to me. I learned to see when writers didn't like their readers; there is a certain voice in much writing that makes apparent its disdain for the reader. Whatever else it had no place in erotic fiction, at least not what we are writing. It would be a mean-spirited piece of fiction that invited someone to share a fantasy that was presented in such a way that the guest was unwelcome.

Numerous forces removed some of the focus of my sexual fiction for a while. They were mainly financial considerations which led me to write a whole body of work that was mercifully published pseudonymously and was most often directed at groups other than gay men. I have written erotic fiction for lesbians, straight men, and straight women. I have worked in what was essentially a porn factory, churning out a required number of pages per week. I have contracted to write entire magazines under a whole list of pen names. I did like some of this; I'm embarrassed by a lot of it; I hope you never discover parts of it.

When people talk about writing pornography as though it were some great ordeal for a writer, they are often referring to situations such as those I've just described, but those are not always as dark as they may seem. There is still the constant use of one's craft and the practice at writing that is invaluable, or can be. It's the sense of frustration at being trapped in such situations that bothers most writers, I think. Unless you are really judging sex and writing about sex with a special heaviness, it is not different than being stuck for a time writing for a hopelessly provincial newspaper while waiting for your skills to be sharpened well enough for you to take advantage of an opportunity to move on, either to a more exciting journal or to a more freewheeling freelance situation.

In any event, I was able to expand what I wrote. I didn't stop writing about sex—far from it—but I increasingly found other pleasure and income writing other types of fiction as well as nonfiction. But wherever I went, the initial experiences of writing pornography remained my foundation as a writer, that thing that gives me a place to stand: I like my readers; I care about their reactions and what is happening to them.

I think my journey has been different than most writers', though I'm hardly unique to have earned a living as a pornographer. Nor did that experience take me to a wholly different place than many other gay writers. Most of us end up in the same arena.

Taken as a group, gay writers do spend more time dealing with sexual issues than do others. There are reasons for it. Gay life treats sex differently. It can be a symbol for self-affirmation—and self-abuse—in a way that often just doesn't translate for other people. A gay man will understand the enormous potential symbolism of being fucked for the first time in a unique way, that it is not an act comparable to losing one's virginity. It can mean much more than that.

Most interestingly, sex is not the end result of an emotional relationship in the gay world, at least not often. That, of course, is the most common depiction of sex in heterosexual and lesbian fiction. Instead, sex is most often the harbinger of emotional relationship that may develop.

We see sex differently. We experience it differently. Often our sex partners are not the most important people in our lives at the moment, but they have the potential of becoming that and our elation when they do—or our response when they don't—informs us of our emotional make-up in a very visceral manner.

More: it is also true that the sex we have is precisely that which initially separates us from the rest of society in the most fundamental way. It is the first essential reason we are alien in this world and therefore it can't be ignored. Its impact is simply too great to be shunted aside.

One of the reasons we constantly return to sex is—I think—that we are always needing to know if this is enough to justify what we go through because of it. Often that's an emotional issue: are these emotions worth it? But because the repercussions are so enormous it becomes a political and social issue as well.

Sex is a part of our identity; it's how we relate to many of the most important people in our lives; it's the vehicle for our most intensely powerful relationships.

It doesn't follow that pornography always addresses all these issues as seriously as it might—not by any means. It could be the equivalent to a Polaroid snapshot of genitalia. Someone would get off on it and it may be sufficient that that photograph helped produce an orgasm to fit the definition. I have taken those photographs and I've written the parallel to them in some pornography. Nor does it follow that sexual writing must deal with all these issues in some intensely analytic fashion—though it might. It is perfectly adequate that it simply be an entertainment.

Sexual writing parallels all the possibilities with which we could deal with sexual activity. We can have sex that's as functional as the shooting of a Polaroid camera or as joyfully uninvolved as a Saturday matinee; we can use it to express our honest emotions or we can laden it with the luggage of our deepest needs.

A while ago I wrote two short stories which appear here—"An Hour's Stopover" and "Authenticity." When I sent each to a magazine editor I received a stronger response from those two men than I ever had before in terms of what he saw in each story.

Those two responses were so direct and so encouraging that I went back and carefully re-read the two pieces. What had I done that could possibly have evoked such a reaction? I then wondered about many of the ideas and much of the history I've told you so far.

I realized that the stories involve a good deal more autobiography than most of my fiction. They are not literal pieces of personal history, but they do relate certain events that honestly intrigued me when they had occurred. I realized too that they weren't loaded with fantasies to cover the specifics. The action wasn't trying to hide conflicting emotions; there were the contradictions that one often finds in a love affair or friendship.

I became more intrigued. I had written enough fiction that I had thought of collecting some in a volume. But there had seldom been a strong foundation that enough stories shared to allow the various pieces to come together as a whole. With the similarity of these pieces, though, I saw more hope. I had a favorite, if mysterious story, "I Once Had a Master," which could serve to set a certain tone, a certain awareness of the vast power and strength that sex might have.

I then set about developing a structure to help me write the stories that could become a book. The progression of a common narrator was an obvious means to part of that. Because sex does mean so many things to me and has had so many purposes I wanted this narrator to have different experiences. There is no one function for sex in my life and no one thing sex symbolizes in my fiction. Here again Sam Steward shows up as a guide.

But I still couldn't find the way to write the equivalent stories that were necessary. I would wander into fantasy, I would go beyond boundaries I wished to keep within. Then it dawned on me: if you will accept the idea that one of the things I like about my writing is that I like the readers, you will be able to understand the importance of this realization.

Each of those two stories had been initially written for a specific person. "An Hour's Stopover" had been written to a particularly delightful arrogant youth. Before I had even considered it for publication it had served another purpose—to lure him into lingering in my life for a while. "Authenticity" had been written as a sort of thank you note to a sweet man who had enriched a Provincetown weekend for me with more emotions than could ever have been defined by the simplistic word "trick."

The stories were an affectionate attempt to look at what had gone on between myself and that one person and to make a gesture to him that I valued the interaction enough to commit my emotional response to paper.

That was what I wanted to do with the rest of the stories, to tell them in a way so specifically directed to various individuals in my life that the richness of the relationships I shared with each might be revealed, not because I wrote the actual journal of events—I haven't—but because the tone of the telling of the tales might display the intimacies. I make no apologies that some of these stories—"Metamorphosis" comes to mind—are not complex with convoluted emotions. Sex as something enjoyed with a friend or else offered as a gift to a companion still falls inside my idea of erotic love.

So, I went about addressing a story to various men in my life. As I looked at the progression that I expected the narrator to make over the twenty years covered in the book I realized that there were signal events, I should say signal individuals, who had marked my own way. I tried to remember them and their impact on me and to write a story to each of them in tones that reflect what occurred to me and what I think might have happened to him.

I don't even know where all of these men are now—I've lost track of some. There is no real history in these stories in any case; all the individuals are carefully shrouded enough that they are not identifiable. I, really, am the only one who needs to know precisely who's involved.

I find this an interesting progression I've undergone: from the beginning as a writer producing sexual work precisely because he hadn't cared about it, hadn't thought it would be taken seriously and therefore hadn't any need to worry about the quality of the writing and its reception, to the place where I can attempt to write sexual fiction of the greatest familiarity.

And it does parallel my existence as a gay man. I am far from that New England boy who hitched the backroads of Massachusetts hoping for an anonymous hand to rest on my thigh. Just as I would find no satisfaction today in taking a Polaroid photograph of a flaccid penis today, so do I insist on more from other men and myself when we share our bodies with one another.

If these stories work it will still be because they are entertaining to you, possibly instructive as well. To some people it may be too voyeuristic to read these tales; the sense that they are being told to someone else, that they were meant for someone else's ears, may be too great. I hope not.

I suppose too that the extent of the sadomasochism may put off some readers. But I couldn't honestly remove that particular smell of sex from these stories once they were being written for specific individuals who would have thought me ignoring reality if I dismissed part of it. They know that our erotic expressions of love were decidedly in that realm.

In any event, they are written. Now I can only do what any writer can—offer them to be read and hopefully enjoyed.

John Preston
Portland, Maine
October, 1983

ABOUT THE AUTHOR

JOHN PRESTON was the author of more than thirty-five books. He was editor of *The Advocate;* his articles and essays appeared in periodicals from *Drummer* to *Harper's* and *Interview*. *I Once Had a Master* comes from a series that includes *Mr. Benson, Entertainment for a Master,* and *Love of a Master.* An activist as well as a writer, Preston founded the first gay and lesbian community center in the United States, in Minneapolis. He died in 1994.